Clover

Barbra Dawson

Copyright © 2023 Barbra Dawson All rights reserved. The characters and events portrayed in this book are fictitious. Any similarity to real persons, living or dead, is coincidental and not intended by the author. No part of this book may be reproduced, or stored in a retrieval system, or transmitted in any form or by any means, electronic, mechanical, photocopying, recording, or otherwise, without express written permission of the publisher. Cover design by: B Dawson

One

As you drive down the main road of Glen Peaks, you may not notice the lack of children in the village. The only sounds that come from here are the soft tinkling bells of a local bakery, the aroma of pastries wafting across its cobblestone walkways and the distant sound of a butcher shop echoing through the streets. You may not notice the quaint river which winds its way through Glen Peaks, passing under ancient stone bridges, slicing through perfectly manicured flowerbeds and vegetable gardens. You wouldn't notice where this river ends - right in front of Hope Cottage's tall grey walls. The cottage's picket fence gate is firmly closed between two walls, with a gleaming brass door knocker beneath its solid oak door. Although it seems invisible to a strangers eye, Hope Cottage stands proudly in its own corner of Glen Peaks.

The night of February 29th, 1984 was a strange one in the village of Glen Peaks. The inhabitants awoke to find the town's oldest house alight with activity - Hope Cottage, secluded deep within its own garden and fields, had come alive. Lights filled every window, spilling out onto the cobbled streets, and smoke billowed from the chimney into the night sky. The elderly townsfolk whispered amongst themselves, their voices intermingled with worry and excitement as they gathered around the cottage. At No 16, Rose spoke excitedly while George of Willow House listened intently. Charlie refused to believe it until he saw it himself. As the townsfolk slowly made their way towards Hope Cottage, those brave enough to venture up the garden path peered through the living room window to find Martha and James, nervously sipping their drinks.

For tonight was the night that the first baby would be born in the village of Glen Peaks. The first baby in 30 years. That night, may just be the night that the curse is broken...

Part 1.
29th February 1984

Two

29th February 1984

The pale moonlight illuminated the small country lane leading to Hope Cottage. Martha and James were all but cocooned by a soft yellow glow emanating from the fireplace in their cosy little cottage. A slight chill had infused the room, despite the bright flames dancing in the hearth. Martha nervously paced the worn hardwood floor, her bare feet brushing against the cold wisps of air that had snuck through the cracks around the window frames. Worry twisted her stomach as her mind raced with anticipation for what was about to come.

Martha shook her head as she uttered the words 'a home birth indeed' under her breath. James stood a few steps away, his hands stuffed in the pockets of his trousers, shifting nervously from foot to foot while Martha repeated the same phrase in a cyclical rant. She held up a finger as if to punctuate her words, emphasizing each one- 'We're in the age of modern medicine, free health care, hospitals with birthing units. Oh James! What if something happens to her up there? What if something goes wrong? What if...' She trailed off and turned to James for comfort, but he had nothing new to offer. He had already told her that everything would be alright countless times.

'It will be grand.' he replied, mustering up a weak smile. Martha noticed the worry lines etched across his forehead and how his hands shook as he filled both their cups with tea, adding an extra spoonful of sugar to hers. 'You know she's been like this throughout the pregnancy, love, you know she'll be fine. Now stop your worrying and come and have a cuppa.'

Martha took her familiar spot on the sofa, but refused to settle in, perched on the edge of her seat instead of sinking into it.

She slowly brought her cup up to her lips and sipped it carefully before setting it back down.

'It's so quiet up there,' she glanced toward the ceiling, as if she could see through it. 'What are they doing up there? And why didn't she let me go in? Anything could be happening. It makes me worry.'

'I've told you, she'll be fine,' James said with an air of forced confidence. He ran his fingers through his hair and avoided Martha's gaze.

'Besides, the midwife is up there. She'll see to her straight.'

Martha shifted her weight and scowled. "The midwife? I don't know if you can call her a midwife anymore. She hasn't practiced in years - you know that."

James could feel his heart sink as he listened to Martha's comment. He knew all too well her doubts about the village midwife that Emma had chosen for the birth of her first child. He wanted to agree with her, but didn't want an argument tonight. His coffee cup shook slightly in his hand as he watched Martha nervously pace the room.

Martha's heartbeat quickened as a muffled sound emerged from the room above. In the time it took for James to place his coffee cup on the table, Martha was already out of the living room and sprinting up the staircase. As Martha vanished from view, a satisfied smile spread across James' face. He finished his coffee and carried the cups into the kitchen before slowly creeping up the stairs after her, giving her five extra minutes of pure bliss.

Martha's footsteps quickened as she hurried up the stairs, where the midwife was just opening the door. The woman beamed proudly and gave her announcement: 'It's a girl! A leap year baby too. Congratulations Granny, or should it be Great Granny?!'

Martha stood frozen with disbelief. She had nine months to prepare for this moment, yet nothing could have prepared her for the surreal feeling of becoming a great grandmother at only sixty-eight years of age. Taking a deep breath, she rushed into the bedroom and found her beautiful granddaughter Emma cradling the newly swaddled bundle of joy.

Martha couldn't contain her excitement as she crossed the room to the bed where Emma lay cradling her new baby. The midwife was admiringly packing away her tools and supplies and praising Emma's performance during the birth, while Martha took in every minute detail of the newborn's face; from the delicate rosy blush of her skin to the tuft of hair already adorning her tiny head. The pride and joy beaming from Emma's smile made Martha's heart swell with love.

James entered just in time to hear Emma proudly announce that they had a baby girl. He made his way slowly over to Martha who was now rocking the little one gently in her arms with a look of pure bliss on her face.

'Come and see James, come and see,' she said with a hint of wonderment in her voice, 'she's the bonniest little thing ever.'

James slowly lifted the blanket from around her face and found a sweet baby girl, fast asleep. Her hair was so fair it almost looked like she had none, and her skin was the perfect shade of pink. She had petite features with a button nose, rosy cheeks, and lips that curved up slightly in the corners. James's heart melted at the sight of her. He glanced over to Emma who looked comfortable and content amidst her new motherhood. A cup of tea rested on her bedside table next to a congratulations card from the midwife.

James bent down and planted a kiss on Emma's forehead before congratulating her on becoming a mum. 'Your Grandma was so worried,' he said with a chuckle as he recalled the hours spent downstairs calming Martha's fears. Emma laughed along with him as he did an impression of Martha marching around the living room.

Martha handed Clover back to Emma before speaking up again. 'Enough about me,' she chided them. 'Have you thought of a name for the poor child?' Emma paused for a moment before revealing the name she had chosen for the sweet baby - Clover – which perfectly reflected the unique personality she would bring to their family.

Martha's eyes widened as she stared at Emma. 'Clover?' she gasped, her hand covering her mouth in disbelief.

'Why not?' Emma shot back; her chin raised defiantly. 'It's no different from Heather or Lily.'

Martha shook her head vehemently. 'But Clover? She'll be teased mercilessly in school,' she protested.

'She's Clover,' Emma insisted, her voice unwavering. James tried to defuse the tension by speaking up. 'Why Clover though? Out of all the names in the world,' he asked, his eyebrows furrowed curiously.

Emma simply glared at him before turning back to Martha and crossing her arms over her chest.

The room fell silent as they all took a moment to process the weight of their disagreement.

'Remember yesterday morning? When I went down to the brook for a walk?' Emma said, her voice filled with elation. Martha watched as Emma's face lit up at the memory. 'It was so warm for the end of February that it almost felt like spring had come early,' She paused, her eyes sparkling as if something extraordinary had happened there. 'Well, I looked down and there, right in front of me, was a four-leaf clover. You know how I've always longed to find one. And what luck would have it, that my daughter would be born on her due date on a leap year? Why, there would be no other name for her but Clover. She'll be the luckiest girl ever.'

Emma smiled dreamily to herself, seemingly transported to a land of fantasy where she imagined her daughter living the life of a luckiest person on Earth. Martha couldn't help but marvel at her immaturity at Twenty-Two; two years more than she was herself when she first became a parent, Emma still held tightly onto childhood dreams. Though she wanted to protest about the chosen name, she couldn't help but think that luck may just be on little Clover's side.

'Well, Clover seems the perfect name,' James said, echoing what they were all thinking.

Three

The next day brought a flood of visitors to Hope Cottage, each arriving with arms full of gifts and eyes bright with anticipation. Martha welcomed them all with gentle smiles and eager hospitality, urging her newfound guests to help themselves to a pot of tea as they made their way into the living room. The cups steadily piled up in the kitchen sink as Martha struggled to keep up with washing them before the next visitor arrived. Emma and Clover stayed put on the sofa, their eyes wide with wonder at the sheer number of people who had come out to celebrate the arrival of new baby Clover. James hurried up and down the lane, restocking supplies of milk and biscuits from the local shop to feed the ever-growing crowd.

'I can't ruddy believe it.' One Farmer boomed, rocking back and forth on his feet as he stood staring at Emma and Clover. Emma couldn't help noticing the smudges of dry mud which had crusted onto his boots and the patches of grass stains which dotted the oversized trousers cinched around his waist. Knowing full well she wouldn't hear the end of it from Martha later in the day for inviting a farmer into Hope Cottage. The farmer had no interest in babies; instead, his typical conversations revolved around farming techniques, crop prices, or gossip about the village. In fact, he had no interest in anything else but himself and his secluded farm, yet there he stood with unabashed admiration for the miracle which was this tiny baby. 'I didn't believe them when I heard the news, so I had to come and see for myself.' Emma smiled to herself. The village were acting like it had been broadcast on the six o'clock news on the BBC.

'I didn't think she'd make it through,' one visitor hissed to another as they stood outside Martha's house. 'What with you know what.'

'Of course, she would have made it,' her neighbourly friend replied confidently. 'She wasn't conceived in the village; she was just born there. Maybe something had gone wrong with you know what.'

Martha refused guests several times throughout the day, granting Emma and baby Clover some much-needed peace and space to feed. In these moments, Martha busied herself around the house, vigorously sweeping floors and running the Ewbank cleaner over rugs while shaking her head about how new mothers needed their rest. Fortunately for them both, Clover took to breastfeeding like a pro; even the midwife commented on how seamlessly it went when she stopped by to check in on them. Motherhood seemed to come naturally to Emma, who cradled little Clover against her chest as she suckled away.

Emma's face softened as she gazed down at her precious newborn laying in her moses basket. Before she could pick her up, the midwife stepped in.

'Now, don't you go holding that baby all the time, mind.' She said in a patronizing tone, offering her advice. 'You don't want to be spoiling her now.'

Emma felt her cheeks flush and pushed back a strand of hair from her face. She took a deep breath before responding.

'Nonsense.' Emma replied firmly. 'She'll have all the cuddles she needs.'

The midwife tutted and studied the floor awkwardly before gathering her things into her midwifery bag.

'I'll be back in a few days to check her weight and see she's doing well. Do take care then.'

After the midwife left, Emma wasted no time springing into action and rummaged through an old chest for some material to make a sling from. With pride, she demonstrated how secure her daughter was in the papoose, snuggled against her chest.

'Nobody gets to tell me how often I should carry my child!' she declared with a triumphant smile.

The local villagers gathered around the village square, whispering amongst themselves about Clover. Mention of a curse seemed to hang in the air, and everyone speculated as to whether it had been lifted with her birth. Rumour had it that the bedroom where she was born was just outside of Glen Peaks, meaning the curse could remain intact. Questions arose as to whether Emma would bear another child or if Clover would stay long enough to have her own young in the village, but nothing could be known for certain.

As the sun set, tendrils of fog began settling among the houses while Martha took her usual seat on her armchair, sighing wearily.

'Well, I never in my life, what a day.' she went on, as Emma passed Clover over to her. Breathing in the sweet scent of the newborn baby - something lost from the village for so long - she let out a little laugh and shook her head. 'I hope tomorrow isn't going to be like today, else I won't have any tea left.'

Emma sat on the floor, marvelling at all the gifts that had been brought for Clover. There were knitted blankets of every colour, old family trinkets that had found themselves without anyone who could give them due care and respect, and even some coins nestled inside cards filled with best wishes.

'She truly is a lucky girl.' Emma said, eyes twinkling in admiration.

'She definitely is.' James agreed as he came in with the unmistakable aroma of fish and chips wafting behind him. 'She's also the talk of the chip shop, and it probably won't surprise you that tonight's tea is on the house. A present for the baby, apparently.'

Martha rolled her eyes at James' offering of fish and chips for the baby, but took the greasy paper bag from him anyway.

'Fish and chips for a baby?' Martha eyed him suspiciously as she stepped aside to let him pass through the doorway.

'Don't go complaining.' James joked. 'Nobody should ever moan about free Fish and Chips. I might just pop into the pub tomorrow and see what's going there.' Martha knew full well he was already planning his next pub trip. Emma observed them fondly from where she held Clover in her arms, feeling lucky that she had these two unique individuals in her life, providing laughter and love for both her and their precious new baby.

Four

As the weeks, months and years passed, Clover's cheerful presence filled the village with joy. The villagers showered her with love in the form of weekly gifts: toys and clothes, sweet treats, and freshly baked goods that arrived at their doorstep. On her birthdays, colourful buntings and balloons adorned the streets while everyone sang and clapped as they watched Clover open her presents. But when she turned two, Emma realized something was wrong - even with the abundance of love and gifts from the village, something was still missing. This became evident one day, as Clover sat enthralled by a children's TV program while Emma worked on house chores with Martha.

'Mama, like me.' Clover pointed out at the other children in the program, all of them her age or older. Her toddler green eyes settled back on her mother. She had lived in the small village all of her short life, but with no local childcare provisions, Emma had been solely responsible for her daughter's care. Sadly, over the last few months, Clover had been forced to watch some of her favourite locals pass away suddenly. Stan, who used to come by every day with a big grin and make Clover giggle uncontrollably, died without warning just six months ago. Not long after him, Ethel – the gentle soul who always went out of her way to make sure Clover was fully kitted out in knitted wear - also passed away unexpectedly. Despite the sadness that filled Emma's heart as she watched her daughter bid farewell to beloved members of their community, it was clear that they had offered tremendous love and kindness to her young daughter. At such an early age, this was a concept Clover could not yet comprehend. Taking a deep breath, Emma knew there was only one thing left to do.

Emma opened the kitchen cupboards, her fingers searching for the dusty old book that held the local directory. She hovered over

Martha, who had settled herself in a creaky chair by the stove, knitting needles clacking as she worked.

'Grandma, where is it?' Emma asked, her voice loud with newfound frustration. 'I need to find playgroups for Clover. She needs friends of her own. Not just us and the people of Glen Peaks!'

Martha looked up from her knitting and sighed. 'Nonsense. Your Grandpa can run around with her.'

'Only for so long before he gets too tired and needs a rest,' Emma countered. 'Besides, she needs other two-year-olds who want to play dress up, have tea parties, and climb trees.'

Martha huffed and tutted as she left the room, resigned to losing another battle against her granddaughter. Emma clenched her jaw in determination as she searched through the piles of books on the shelf until finding the one, she was looking for; its yellowing pages already flipped open to the appropriate section. Running her finger down the 'P' page, she quickly found the subsection; 'Playgroups.' There were seven listed within the county.

Grabbing a pen and paper from a nearby cabinet, Emma wrote down the phone numbers of three of the most local ones, hoping that they would still be running. Ensuring Clover was still transfixed with the television and absorbed in making imaginary food for her stuffed animals, Emma slipped out into the hallway and began calling each of the contact numbers.

Emma cautiously dialled the first number and was greeted by a cheerful woman on the other line. After she outlined her enquiries, the woman eagerly provided her with all the information Emma needed to know about the playgroup. She hung up, pleased with herself and feeling smug, just as Martha walked past, carrying an overflowing basket of laundry in her arms.

'Well?' Martha asked with a tone of expectation, prompting Emma to explain.

'I rang three places and they all run on different days. So, I'm taking Clover to the first one tomorrow morning.' Emma declared triumphantly.

Martha looked at her in disbelief and shook her head. 'Don't tell me you're going to take her to all three?' she said incredulously.

'Of course, I am! Grandma!' Emma grinned mischievously. 'That way we can figure out which one we like best.'

Without another word, Martha continued on her way, leaving behind a single errant sock from the pile of washing she was carrying. Feeling a small hand slip into hers from behind her, Emma looked down to find Clover standing there - big green eyes twinkling in anticipation and golden curls dancing around her bright face.

'We go see Katie now?' Clover asked excitedly, referring to one of the residents in the village.

'We'll see Katie now.' Emma confirmed. 'Go get your shoes and your coat.'

Emma could not help but smile as she watched Clover bounce off to get her belongings.

Clover's tiny fists pounded rhythmically on Katie's door, growing louder with each knock. A smile tugged at the corners of Emma's mouth as Clover looked up at her expectantly, her little body wriggling in anticipation of what was to come.

'Who's at the door?' Katie's voice came from within the house and Clover dissolved into a fit of giggles.

'No! Knock, Knock, Knock!' she shouted back.

'Who's at the door?' Katie replied again, her voice closer now as if she had been teasingly prolonging their game. 'Is it the milkman?'

Clover squealed with delight and shouted back, 'No! Knock, Knock, Knock!'

Katie's hand pressed down on the door handle, her emerald eyes twinkling with anticipation. 'I know who it is!' she called out one last time, just as the door opened to reveal Clover standing there, enthusiasm bursting from every part of her being. 'It's me!' she cried, bouncing with excitement.

'Well, well, well, I didn't expect it to be you!' Katie grinned back knowingly and waved them into her small cottage. A real brick fireplace blazed in the centre of the living room surrounded by an assortment of furniture and trinkets that gave the room a cosy feel, immediately encouraging Emma to sink into the armchair. Katie and Clover then disappeared into the adjoining kitchen to find the biscuit barrel before emerging with a tray complete with teapot and cups, and Clover proudly carrying her favourite gold-tin covered biscuit barrel decorated with cats sitting in a country garden - already a few biscuits missing from it.

'So, what have we been up to today?' Katie asked warmly, after pouring them both a cup of tea.

'Me play playdough.' Clover announced proudly. 'Me do drawing!'

'How lovely, and what did you draw?'

'Me draw Mama and grandy and gramma'.

Emma smiled to herself, the way Clover had always pronounced the names for Grandad and Grandma had always melted her. She hoped they'd always be Grandy and Gramma.

'And what has Mama been up to?' Katie focused her attention on Emma as she passed the tea over.

'Actually, I've phoned some playgroups this afternoon.'

'And I bet Martha didn't like that.' Katie guessed before Emma could even explain.

'Not exactly, no, but I really feel it's time for Clover to make friends of her own.' She glanced down at Clover, who was now colouring in a book that was specifically kept on Katie's coffee table.

'And I think you are completely right. When my Nicholas was Clover's age, we were forever at the village hall either watching them play or having birthday parties. Besides, it won't be long before Clover starts school and you don't want that to be the first time she sees children of her own age.'

Emma knew that talking to Katie was the best thing to put her mind at ease, she just hoped that it really was the best decision.

Five

Emma and Clover stood huddled together at the bus stop, the morning sun warming their faces. A light chill hung in the air, and wisps of steam rose from their breath. Emma surveyed Clover with a sharp eye, noting her freshly laundered corduroy dress, embroidered flowers stitched along the bottom seam. It was one of Clover's favourite dresses, a birthday gift from Mary-Ann; however, there had been few opportunities for wearing it outside of the village. Her curls were perfect ringlets today after a morning bath. Clover fidgeted nervously as they waited for their bus into the next town. She chewed on her bottom lip until Emma bent down and placed a kiss atop her head.

'Bus coming now?' Clover asked surveying the empty road ahead.

'It'll be here soon,' Emma replied reassuringly. 'And then we will make lots of new friends - exactly like you! And they will all love you.'

Clover's eyes lit up with anticipation as the bus rumbled around the corner and pulled to a stop. Emma inhaled sharply as Clover stepped forward, her small frame tensed with excitement.

'Bus coming now,' Clover announced loudly.
As the bus came to a stop, Dale - the regular driver swung open the heavy doors and welcomed them aboard. His bright blue eyes sparkled beneath his bus driver's cap as he asked their destination.

'Well, good morning to two beautiful ladies.' He grinned. 'Where are you off to today?'

'Me go playgroup!' Clover exclaimed with a hint of nervousness in her voice, but she smiled all the same. 'Me make lots of friends.'

Dale chuckled to himself as he took the bus fare from Emma. 'And that I'm sure you will, young Clover, and they will love you just as much as we all do.'

Clover beamed with a grin as she took in Dale's compliments. Taking their places in the empty seats, Clover turned to Emma.

'Hope they love me.'

'The certainly will,' Emma reassured her. 'We'll be there soon, and then you'll see. I wonder what toys will be there for you to play with?'

'Me like stickle bricks,' Clover replied. 'Hope friends like stickle bricks.'

They spent the rest of the journey gazing out of the window, Clover pointing and exclaiming in delight at the world in motion beyond. Emma's thoughts drifted to their destination - would her daughter fit in with this new group, with these other children she had not met before? Would she remember how to share and take turns? The questions rolled around her head like a carousel, her heart sinking at each rotation. Just then, Dale called out for them to disembark, and Emma took a deep breath as they stepped off the bus.

'Come on you. Let's go play,' Emma said, as she helped Clover down from her seat and made her way to the front of the bus.

Luckily, the village hall where Cherished Playgroup was run from was right across the road from the bus stop.

'This it?' Clover asked, looking across the road, and spotting a child who looked her age entering the hall. 'Look mama!' she pointed out.

'This is it,' Emma confirmed, spotting a poster hanging from the railings which clearly said *'Cherished Playgroup here. Every Wednesday. 9.30-11.30.'*

They walked hand in hand and were greeted by Hazel the minute they walked through the door.

'Oh, my! And who is this delightful little thing?' Hazel asked. With such excitement in her voice, Emma questioned whether she had ever seen a child before.

'This is Clover.' Emma replied. 'I called yesterday. I'm Emma.'

Hazel ran a finger down the lines of names on her clipboard, her lips mouthing each one until she found the one she was looking for. 'Clover,' she said, her eyes lighting up with recognition. 'Ah, yes, you must have spoken to Ann yesterday.'

She waved them forward, and Emma noticed Clover hang back slightly as they entered the hall. The air hummed with the excited shouts of children at play, accompanied by an undertone of laughter and conversation from where the parents were gathered around a low table at the other end of the room. Hazel led them over.

'You can help yourself to tea or coffee over there.' she pointed as they made their way over. 'And the toilets are just to the left of the entrance you came in.'

Emma could see the parents stuck in a variety of chat and felt embarrassed as Hazel introduced both her and Clover to them.

'Girls, this is Emma and Clover,' she announced, making them turn their heads and look. 'They're joining us this morning to see if they like it.'

A few of the mums smiled and gave a slight wave. One of them was breastfeeding one of their children, so with both hands full, gave a slight nod of the head. Hazel pulled a chair out and made space at the table. Emma took it as her cue to take a seat.

'I'm Jane.' the mum closest to her announced. 'My children are off over there.' she pointed into the small crowd of children sat at a table with building blocks. 'That's Jack with the black hair and red jumper. Opposite him is my youngest Sophie, in the pink dress and then my eldest is the one wearing the hat. That's Bobby'.

Emma took a double glance at the woman sat next to her, who barely looked not even a few years older than herself and wondered how it was possible she already had three children.

'I know what you're thinking,' Jane interrupted her thoughts. 'Everyone thinks the same. Three children at my age, eh? Well, me and the dad are childhood sweethearts. We knew we wanted a big family, and let's just say, we started as soon as we could. If you get what I mean.'

'How lovely,' was all Emma thought to reply. Secretly, the thought of having three children so young filled her with dread.

'I'm Claire,' said another parent, joining them. She leaned across the table, placing a cup of tea down in front of Emma. 'I take it Jane has just filled you in on her ever-growing brood. Just the one for me is enough.' she laughed. 'So, tell us about yourself. I don't recall seeing you around the town?'

'Oh, I'm not from here,' Emma began, as she stirred sugar into her tea. 'I'm living in Glen Peaks at the moment with my grandparents. I only moved back just before Clover was born. I lived in Brighton with my mother before that for the last 15 years.'

'Glen Peaks?' the mother who was breastfeeding quizzed. 'I've never heard of it. Where's that then?'

'You know it,' Claire explained. 'That little village in between Harrington and Hoyle. If you take the first left, the minute you leave Harrington, it takes you right down into Glen Peaks. Although I'll be honest with you, Emma, I didn't even know there was anything there. I've heard some right rumours about that place.'

Emma sipped her tea, despite it being too hot. This was one problem she thought she'd encounter.

'Still don't know it,' breastfeeding mum claimed. 'But go on, what rumours?'

'Well,' Claire began, as she leaned back into her chair, hands cupped around her coffee. 'Thirty years ago, although it seems to have been thirty for a while now. So, let's say thirty-five years ago, an old widow placed a curse on the town. Apparently, the whole town outcast her, that's why. She was forever alone, friendless, no husband and no children. She was certain that her misfortune was all down to the people of the village. If they had accepted her, then she could have lived a very normal life. Well, the story goes she watched the town's people from her house every day and saw the joy which their families brought them. The joy she was forever missing. Therefore, she took it upon herself to cast a curse that no child was ever be born within Glen Peaks again. And from that day forward, no child has ever been conceived. Have you never driven through it and thought it odd that it's all old people? No schools or toy shops, not a park or a single child playing.'

Emma had heard the tale all too often. She knew the legend of the village; the stories told as people mentioned Glen Peaks.

'Is this true?' breastfeeding mum asked her directly.

'It can't be true,' Claire interrupted before Emma could reply. 'After all, Clover and Emma are from Glen Peaks, and unless Emma has some magical anti-aging cream, we're not using. She's definitely under 35 years.'

'Let her speak,' breastfeeding mum scolded. 'Go on, what do you think, Emma?'

Emma ran her fingers around the rim of her steaming mug, lost in thought. Memories from long ago flooded in - of growing up in a home filled with vibrant colours and an air of mystery. Her mother had been the kind of person who beliefs were set firmly in superstition, believing that certain rituals could bring luck, ward off evil, and encourage good fortune. She recalled helping her mother hang dream catchers above the windowsills, place crystals on the mantelpiece, and tuck worry dolls beneath pillows as they brushed their teeth at bedtime. Even though Emma wasn't quite sure she believed in all the traditions just yet, she couldn't help but appreciate how it had shaped her thoughts and outlooks on life. Wasn't it a lucky coincidence that they'd found a four-leaf clover just before her daughter was born? It was almost as if the universe was telling them to name their daughter Clover. And hadn't there always been a whisper about a mysterious witch living nearby her grandparents when she was younger? Whenever she asked about it, her grandparents changed the subject quickly.

'Well, I'm not sure.' Emma finally said, opting for the safe route so as not to seem too strange to the group. 'Nobody even knows who the witch was supposed to have been? Besides, I reckon there's been no babies born in the village for so long, as most of the children grew up and moved away to the local cities, like my mother. Nobody new ever moves to Glen Peaks anymore.'

'That sounds like a perfect explanation.' Claire seemed pleased. Emma gauged quickly that Claire didn't like the thought of anything supernatural.

'Besides,' Emma continued. 'I wasn't born in Glen Peaks, and I did not conceive Clover there, she was just born there.'

'Clover?' breastfeeding mum interrupted again. 'That's an odd name.'

'I'm the luckiest girl there was.' Clover, who had still been sat on Emma's knee the whole time, burst out with pride. Most of the other woman laughed at Clover. However, breastfeeding, mum cast a scornful look.

'I'm sure you are,' she tutted to herself, before removing her daughter from her breast and placing her back into her pram.

Six

When they arrived home, Martha was bustling about in the kitchen, so Emma and Clover made their way out to the garden where James was tinkering in the greenhouse. "Grandy!" Clover exclaimed as she pulled open the door.

James turned toward them, and his face lit up with a wide smile. 'Oh, there you are. I thought you'd got lost!' He produced a bunch of small red tomatoes from behind his back and offered it to Clover with a playful wink. 'Don't tell Grandma; you know what she'd say!'

Clover mimicked Martha's stern voice: 'It will ruin our tea!'

Emma couldn't help but smile at the scene in front of her—she loved how close Clover and James always were. He scooped up some empty plant pots and handed them to her and then grabbed several small tools from the shelf and set off for the shed. 'Come on you two—help me tidy up here, we best get inside for tea. Then you can tell me all about your day.'

Martha sat down at the kitchen table and surveyed the meal she had just cooked. She glanced over as Emma and Clover entered the room. 'So, how was it?' she asked, noting the streaks of dirt on Emma's clothes from helping James outside.

Emma sunk into a chair exhaustion evident on her face. 'Oh, it was very nice,' she replied as she tucked into her food. 'I chatted with some of the other parents, they all seem lovely.'

Clover jumped in, eyes sparkling, 'Mummy, talk about witch!' Martha suppressed a look of disgust as Emma nearly choked on her piece of meat.

'Oh, I see.' Martha replied smiling at Clover, whilst casting a glance at Emma. 'Mummy, enjoys telling stories, doesn't she?'

Clover nodded eagerly in agreement. After all, Emma was always making up stories for her. Whether they went on a bear hunt down the meadow or finding fairies and letting them go in the springtime as the dandelions took over the garden.
'Make a wish.' Emma would always tell her as she blew the fairies away.

Emma knew the importance of expanding a child's imagination and, besides, making walks more exciting by making an adventure of them, made them much more enjoyable.

'Did you like the playgroup, Clover?' Martha asked Clover. Emma watched with anticipation. They'd talked about the playgroup on the bus on the journey home. Clover had expressed how she had enjoyed the group; however, Emma wasn't too sure she was simply telling Emma what she wanted to hear.

Clover began to explain: 'We went bus. Me saw Dale!' She remembered each detail with childish enthusiasm, as if sharing a great adventure, her little hands fluttering in excitement as she recited every detail of their time there.

'I bet Dale enjoyed having you on his journey.' Martha replied. 'Did you like the playgroup?'

'Clover got biscuits!'

'How lovely! Did you play with any toys?'

'Did colouring when mummy talk of witch.'

'And when we go back next week, maybe you can play with some children too?' Emma interrupted the conversation as the house phone rang in the background. James stood and ambled towards the hallway where the phone hung on a wall; his chubby hands tugging at his faded jeans as he walked. As he answered it, Emma heard his cheery tune, so familiar that she could imagine Santa himself on the other end of the line.

'Emma, it's for you!' he boomed through the house. Confused about who would be calling her, she pushed her chair away from the table, leaving Martha and Clover to continue their conversation.

Gripping the cold plastic receiver tightly in her hands, Emma hesitantly uttered a hello into the phone.

'Emma?' the voice on the end of the phone replied. 'I'm so glad I got the right number!'

Emma tried to place the voice on the other end, but her memory failed her.

'Hazel gave me your number. I really hope you don't mind?' the voice continued. 'It's Claire, by the way. Claire from the playgroup, with Emily.'

Emma's mind raced as she tried to place her caller. Then the memory of a blonde woman with unruly hair she knew who it was.

'Claire?' Emma asked cautiously. She wondered why Claire would be calling her. Exchanging an awkward silence, Emma tensed up until Claire began to apologize on behalf of Debbie, the stuck-up woman at their last gathering. 'Debbie?' Emma questioned, not quite understanding what Debbie had to do with anything.

Claire tittered awkwardly before continuing, 'No no, Debbie isn't actually why I'm calling you today. You see, I got a really good feeling about you and Clover and wanted to arrange a playdate between us.' Emma felt confused for a moment before realizing that Emily was about Clover's age, and this could be a great opportunity for them both to make friends. She breathed out heavily and nodded into the phone.

'Absolutely.' Emma replied, her mind already rushing through a list of days and times that would work. 'I think that sounds like a great plan! When did you want to arrange for?'

Claire hesitated as she thought over her schedule. 'Well, I'm free any day really, apart from Saturdays. Friday afternoons I always go into town and do a bit of shopping.'

'How about tomorrow?' Emma almost interrupted, eager to make the plans so she could tell Clover about them.

'Tomorrows perfect.' Claire beamed down the phone, her enthusiasm obvious even through the phone line. 'I can't wait to go and tell Emily; she and Clover will get on like a house on fire. I can feel it.'

'Right, well I'll see you tomorrow then.' Emma quickly bid goodbye to Claire, who seemed content in making small talk despite the tightness of their conversation before.

Making her way back into the dining room, she was looking forward to telling her daughter about her new friend. She hoped that both Clover and Martha would immediately take to Emily.

Seven

Emma sighed as she sorted through Clovers wardrobe, struggling to keep her frustration in check. Martha's clattering echoed up the stairs from the kitchen below, and Emma heard her muttering something about visitors at such short notice. She hadn't thought twice when she had suggested they meet tomorrow; after all, it was Emma's day off with no plans, and Claire had her own car so they wouldn't need to rely on buses.

'Emily play swings?' Clover asked, interrupting Emma as she pulled out a pair of dungarees.

'I'm sure she'd love to play on the swings with you.' Emma replied cheerfully, she couldn't wait for Clover to finally have another child to play with.

Fastening up Clover's dungarees they both headed downstairs.

Martha was in full swing, frantically fussing over everything in sight. She had already plumped the cushions on the couch, dusted every nook and cranny of the room, and baked a delicious spread of treats for their guest's arrival. Emma spotted James dragging his muddy shoes across the hallway floor and quickly rescued Martha from yet another disaster by sweeping up the mess before she noticed.

'Ah Emma, you're finally ready.' Martha said as she turned around just as the mess was disposed. 'Right, I've done a coffee cake, a fruit cake and made some scones. There are also some cheese straws for the children. The tea is in the pot waiting so you'll just need to boil the kettle when she gets here.'

'Really Grandma, you've done too much, a plate of biscuits and a cup of tea would have been just fine.'

'You can't go offering guests a plate of biscuits. Really Emma, you invite this woman into our home, and you want to offer her a plate of biscuits? What kind of impression do you intend on making?'

Emma found it ironic how she was set against Clover making friends and now was trying to impress the very one they had made.

Their conversation was interrupted as Clover bounced through the hall, skipping along with her arms piled with toys.

'Getting toys ready for Emily.' She announced proudly, carrying them through to the kitchen.

Martha couldn't disagree that it would be nice to see Clover playing with children of her own age. She tutted to herself, not allowing her change of attitude to be noticed and continued dusting. Emma walked through, following Clover, picking up stray toys as she went through. Sure, enough laid out on the table were a variety of cakes, Clover had even set out her toy tea set for everyone.

'Be here soon?' Clover questioned. Emma glanced at the clock above the aga oven.

'They will be. See when that big hand points to the very top?' Clover nodded eagerly.

'That's when they'll be here.'

Emma could only hope that Claire was a punctual person and wouldn't keep Clover waiting.

※※※※※

'Mummy, here, here, here!' Clover started shouting, as she watched Claire's car pull into the driveway. Before she knew it, Clover had pulled on her wellies which didn't match her princess dress she had insisted on changing into and was running out onto the driveway to greet them. Clover ran straight over to Emily, helping her out of the car and taking her hand.

'Hello!' Clover shouted excitedly waving her arms in greeting too.

'You found us alright then?' Emma asked, just as Claire helped Emily out of the car and the two girls ran off to no doubt, see Clover's favourite tree swing.

'Oh yes, found it perfect thanks, your directions were spot on.'

Claire followed Emma into the house, where Martha was already boiling the kettle, despite her insistence that she would make herself scarce.

'Claire, this is my grandmother Martha.' Emma introduced.

'How lovely to meet you Martha and thank you so much for letting us pop over and visit. Emily has been excited all morning.'

'Oh, it's no problem at all, it's so nice to see Clover having another child to play with, I'm sure they'll soon become the best of friends.'

Emma raised her eyebrows behind Claires back, just enough for Martha to see. Considering the conversations that had been happening between them both over the last couple of days, Martha seemed to have changed her tone.

'You two enjoy a rest in here, I'm going to go out into the garden and keep an eye on everyone while they play,' Martha said as she fixed herself a cup of tea. Emma watched as Martha headed out to the back garden where James was already spinning the girls around on the swing hung from one of the trees. Their delighted laughter drifted up and filled the valley with joy.

Claire stood beside Emma and stared out at the scene of bliss in front of them. 'It's so beautiful here,' she finally said. 'You are so lucky that Clover has all this land she can explore. With Emily, we're pretty much limited to our small flat or going out for walks and trips to the park.'

'Yes, it is quite idyllic. They've lived in this house for years, my mother grew up here, and I loved visiting for the holidays when I was younger. The place hasn't changed a bit. We'll let them have a play and then maybe we'll take you on a walk and show you the sights. There's a brook at the bottom of the garden, where Clover loves to play Pooh Sticks.'

'Sounds perfect!' Claire smiled back.

The first nerves Emma felt, inviting Claire into their home, was worrying if the girls would fall out or not get on. Equally worrying was if her and Claire would find enough to talk about, instantly evaporated. The girls were more alike than Emma could ever imagined, and Clover accepted her like a long-lost friend. Claire spoke enough for both and didn't seem to run out of any topics of conversation that it wasn't until Clover and Emily burst through the kitchen door, asking for cake, that Emma had noticed they'd been playing out for an hour already. Emma and Claire helped the girls up onto the chairs around the table, and they helped themselves to the cupcakes which Martha had made and decorated for them earlier that morning,

'We take Katie some cake later?' Clover asked.

'Yes, I suppose we could do, she does love a slice of cake.' Emma smiled back.

'Who's Katie?' Claire asked Clover.

'Katie my friend.' Clover replied, and before Emma could interrupt, Clover looked up, smiled and asked, 'Emily see Katie too?'

Emma worried herself earlier, as to whether Clover would talk about her elderly friends in the village. Worried of how Claire and Emily may respond.

'We would love to see Katie.' Claire agreed, 'Does she live nearby?'

'Live number 8.' Clover replied confidently.

'And how old is Katie?'

'Katie old, like grandma.'

'Well, she sounds lovely! Will she be in if we visit?'

'Katie always in.'

'Let's go see Katie!' both girls chorused together.
Emma smiled, over her cup of tea, not sure how her new guests will perceive one of Clovers dearest friends.

As they traipsed through the village, the sun bore down on their backs as they passed the quaint little cottages that made up the sleepy hamlet. With a proud smile, Emma pointed out the village hall – her mother's old primary school – and the disused sweet shop where she used to buy sweets as a child.

'And where did the witch used to live?' Claire asked. Emma didn't really want to divulge the topic of conversation so tried to keep it as brief as possible.

'We'll be going past it soon, there's a small cottage next to the butchers, it's run down, and nobody has lived in there for as long as I can remember.'

'So, you think it's true then? All this witch and curse talk?'

'Who's to know? There's simple reasoning as to why nobody has had children in the village, most of them being that those of childbearing age had moved out of the village to seek better opportunities and the residents here just stayed once their own child had grown up.'

'Well, who used to live in the cottage? Do you know?'

'I've never looked into it, Martha and James don't really like to talk about it, and I've never really heard anyone else mention it. It's my mother who told me where she supposedly lived.'

'And what about Clover? She was born here fine.'

'Well Clover was conceived outside of the village, so really, I think if the curse was real, then that wouldn't apply, would it?'

Claire shrugged, unsure what to say.

'So, what about Clover's father? How come you're living here?'

This was another question Emma knew would eventually come up whenever she tried to make friends.

'There's not really a story to tell. Mum moved to Bristol with my dad before I was born. Their marriage didn't last, so we lived in a 2-bedroom flat. Bad mistakes happen, and I ended up with an unplanned, unexpected pregnancy. The father made it clear that he wanted no part, and I wanted to escape, so I ended back here months before Clover was born. The plan was to stay for the birth and until I was settled, yet here I am, and I love it here. I'll have to get a job soon though, especially when Clover starts school, so may need to move out of the village.'

'You should learn to drive.' Was all Claire replied with, luckily before any of the conservation could be extended on, they had already reached the gate of Katies house and Clover was already started to knock on the door, trying to hold back the giggles for what was to come when Katie replied.

Eight

2 years later

Dressed in her tartan pinafore, with her white shirt underneath, Clover looked picture perfect ready for her first day at school.

'I hope I make some new friends.' Clover mentioned, as Emma brushed her hair into a ponytail.

'I'm sure you'll make lots of friends and remember Emily will be there too.'

'Me and Emily are best friends.' Clover announced proudly.

'You certainly are, but always make sure that if you do make new friends, you include Emily too. It wouldn't be nice to make her feel left out.'

With a few nimble fingers, Emma delicately braided Clover's hair into a neat ponytail, adorned with a matching tartan bobble. Clover beamed with excitement at her new look in the mirror and spun around like a ballerina, making her brand-new school uniform twirl. Emma smiled fondly as she watched her daughter, who was ready to face the world.

'Perfect. Come on let's go say bye to Granny and Grandad.' Heading into the kitchen, they found James admiring their handiwork. 'My, don't you look smart – you'll knock 'em off their feet!' he said, causing Clover to light up with joy.

Martha was standing by the window, watching them quietly. Her glassy eyes betrayed the sadness that had been lingering for weeks now that it was time for Clover to begin school and leave the comfort of home. Even though Emma was eager for this new chapter in their lives, she couldn't help but feel a pang of sorrow knowing that she would miss having her daughter around all the time. But it also meant new beginnings for Emma.

'You two better get a move on.' Martha said handing Clover her lunch bag, 'Here you go, I've made you some little treats in there, along with your favourite sandwich. And here's a little gift for you.'

Clover took the small package which Martha had handed her and opened it. Clover gasped as she pulled out a small silver bracelet, with a small four-leafed clover attached.

'I love it.' Clover beamed, leaning in to give Martha a hug.

'Ah, it's just a little good luck gift. Not that you'll need it.'

'Come on you.' Emma interrupted, as Martha wiped her eyes. 'We need to get going or we'll be late.'

Emma picked up the set of car keys from the fruit bowl. After taking Claire's advice all those years ago learning how to drive really was the best decision she'd made. Luckily, she passed just a few months ago, just in time to take Clover to the nearest school, which was five miles away.

'You know where you're going?' James quizzed.

'Of course, I do, and I know where to park.' Emma added, before James could ask any more questions.

'Well on you get then. You don't know what the traffic can be like getting into Hazel Cross at this time of the day.'

Emma made one last check to ensure Clover had everything she needed for her first big day and set off.

※※※※※

Clover sprinted through the school gates, her shoes clapping against the concrete path and echoing off the school walls. She spotted Emily and Claire huddled together near a tree, both with red eyes, tear tracked cheeks, and an empty expression.

As she reached them, Emily jumped back slightly, burying herself deeper into Claire's clothes. Emma crouched down to meet her eye level and softly asked, 'Are you okay?'

'She's feeling just a bit nervous about starting I think.' Claire replied, trying to sound positive and not letting the crack in her voice show.

'You can have my lucky penny.' Clover said, taking out the penny she'd found outside of the school gates. 'Grandma always says, find a penny, pick it up, all day long you'll have good luck. And I don't need it, as I have my lucky bracelet.'

The penny glinted in the sunlight as Emily took it and clasped it in her fist, the metal surprisingly warm amidst the cool autumn air. Clover smiled up at her brightly and said, 'You'll have good luck all day now.'

'Reception children this way please.' The voice of their new teacher echoed across the playground, calling for reception children to make their way over to her. Parents began to herd their children towards the teacher, some having to physically pry their children away from them, much to their dismay. Butterflies fluttered in Emily's stomach as she looked up at Clover and shakily smiled back. But then Clover grabbed hold of her hand firmly, her lucky penny still clutched in the other one, and they walked across the playground together until they were swallowed up by the school building.

Emma and Claire waited until all the children had completely vanished from view and the school doors were shut.

'I told her I'd wait her for her.' Claire sighed, bemused at the white lie's parents tell their children for an easier life. 'Obviously to try and make her feel better, but now I find myself not wanting to leave.'

'I know how you feel.' Emma replied. 'I'd love nothing more than to go and sneak in to see how they're doing.'

'But here we are, our new life, where for 6 hours of the day we don't' know how they are or what they're doing. I think I'm gonna need another baby.' Claire Laughed, trying to make light of the situation.

'Or a dog,' Emma laughed back. 'Definitely get a dog, or cat.'

'Come on, let's go, before we know it, we'll be back here and moaning that we haven't had time to do what we wanted because we've been too busy sulking.'

Nine

4 Years later

'Mum, I want to go!' Clover pleaded, following Emma through the house as she picked up piles of washing which Martha's arthritic hands could no long do.

'I've told you Clover, I really don't think it's the right thing.'

Emma hurriedly scooped the pile of clothes from the dining table and deposited them into a dark corner of the kitchen. The aroma of freshly washed laundry lingered in the air as she quickly filled the kettle with water and set it to boil. James would be needing a cup of tea soon and after his stroke the previous year, Emma didn't like to give him the opportunity to handle the boiling water himself.

'Plus, I would really appreciate it, if you could stay home and help Grandma if she needs the help.'

Martha, being Martha didn't like accepting the help, but Emma noticed daily the pain the arthritis caused her as she tried to do any manual work around the house. She'd witnessed the pain etched across her face, as she lifted even a cup of tea. Despite her denying that she was in any discomfort at all, it was clear to see in many ways.

'But we won't be gone for long, if we make sure everything is done before hand, I'll help, I promise.'

Emma could see the tears threatening to burst in Clovers green eyes.

'She was my friend too Mum, please.'

Emma sighed, as she poured out the tea into the same bone China cups they'd always used. She knew these times would come, and it broke her heart as much as anyone else's. Especially as Clover pointed out, Katie was her friend too. Despite her eight years of life, the little girl had shown an extraordinary maturity and a strong devotion to their beloved friend; whether it was running down after school for a quick chat or stopping by the shops to gather supplies, she never missed a chance to catch up with Katie. Emma knew how hard this would be for Clover and finally conceded that she also deserved to attend Katie's funeral.

'Alright, but you need to make sure there's nothing in this house that needs doing before we go. I don't want Grandma or Grandpa doing anything when we're gone.'

Clover smiled, and quickly headed off, no doubt to make a start on any chores, to be ready for the funeral tomorrow morning.

Emma looked out at her now, rusty car on the drive which had just four years ago promised her and Clover freedom and a new life. The voice of her own mother echoed in her memory. *'If you go back there, you'll be stuck there for the rest of your life.'* She'd said, when Emma had announced she was off to Glen Peaks to give birth to Clover. It was only supposed to be a temporary arrangement and once Clover had started school; Emma started to retrain as a nurse. Her future was really looking bright, and she was even looking at renting her own place closer to Clover's school. That all changed the day James had his stroke. Martha found him in the garden, as she went out to hang out the washing. Unfortunately, due to the location of Glen Peaks an ambulance took longer than it should have done. James' recovery was slow with irreversible damage. Emma soon found herself, postponing her life and took on the role of carer for both of her grandparents.

The shrill ringing of the phone cut through the silence in the cottage.

'Phone,' James shouted from the lounge, poking his head around the doorframe with a look of confusion on his face. He dragged one leg behind him as he hurriedly walked back to the living room and plopped himself down onto the chair with a huff.

'I'm coming,' Emma called back as she turned off the boiling kettle and moved towards the hallway.

'Hope Cottage,' Emma answered, emotions shifting between love and heartache at hearing her mother's voice again. She had been absent for so long that it seemed strange to still hear her calling in such frequency since James' stroke.

'Emma, Darling, are you there?'

'Is it?' James shouted from the living room; his pronunciation still not fully complete.

'Emma, Darling, are you there?'

'Hang on,' Emma said down the phone before covering the receiver and shouting into James. There was only a grunt in response.

'Yes mother, I'm here.' Emma replied. 'I'm back. Is everything ok?'

Emma's mothers voice was low and serious. 'I had my tarot cards read today,' she said. Emma rolled her eyes, trying to restrain herself from interrupting. But then her mother's words hit her like a brick wall – 'I think it's time I come back. I'm coming back to Hope Cottage, Emma.' Her mouth went dry as the weight of her mother's statement sank in.

Emma fell silent, dumbstruck as to what to say. Emma had grown up with moans of Hope Cottage and the village. Of how it had nothing that the big cities had. How she never wanted to be the model stay-at-home parent, and run a house, or be tied down to marriage.

'Emma, did you hear me? I don't know if the line is all funny.'

'Er, yes, I did. What do you mean you're coming back?'

'Like I said, I'm coming back to Hope Cottage. I think it's time. The Tarot Cards said about me needing to see family as important and going back to my old roots will help new beginnings.'

'Okay...' Emma replied slowly. 'And when are you moving back?'

'I've given notice on the flat, and I need to be gone a week tomorrow.' She replied confidently. 'Oh Em, it will be so much fun, it will be like when we lived together again.'

Emma had those memories, but they seemed to be a slightly different version than her mothers. Emma had also noticed, that despite her Tarot Cards supposedly declaring the importance of family, her mother had still yet failed to ask anything of Clover or of Martha and James. Deep inside, Emma hoped she now wasn't going to the be carer of yet another person.

Emma hung up the phone, just as Clover walked past.

'Who was that?' Clover asked.

'That was your grandma,' Emma replied with a sigh.

Clover peeked around the doorframe, confused as to why her grandmother would be on the phone.

'What, Grandma June?'

'The one and only. She's coming to stay.'

Clover had only met her grandmother a couple of times in passing, and contact between them both had been minimal.

'For how long?' Clover quizzed, hoping against hope that it wouldn't be bad news.

'Apparently forever,' Emma replied, shaking her head in disbelief. She knew this meant breaking the news to Martha and James, which could prove difficult.

Suddenly feeling trapped, Emma took a deep breath as she braced herself for what was to come.

Ten

The walk through the church yard was breathtaking. The sun glimmered through the blossom trees, their delicate petals creating an inviting path of pink and white. Petals blanketed the ground like confetti, drifting away with every breeze that blew.

'They look so pretty.' Clover admired. 'Katie would have loved them.'

Emma smiled back at her. She was right of course, Katie loved anything pink coloured and was always admiring the pink rose bush planted in her front garden.

'Pink was her favourite colour.' Clover reminded Emma. Which was why Clover was dressed in her favourite pink dress. Refusing to follow the general rule of wearing black to a funeral. She'd simply stood her ground while getting ready that morning.

'Katie wouldn't want you to be all sad and in black.' She'd demanded and truth be told, Emma knew she was completely right.

As Emma and Clover approached the small group of guests gathered at the entrance of the church, she could make out familiar faces from old photographs scattered around Katie's home. Though they had lived in the same village for eight years, Emma had never seen these people before, nor had Katie ever spoken of them visiting. Her heart sank as she watched the group share fond memories of her late friend--memories that none of them truly understood.

'Ah! Here she is!' The Church Vicar exclaimed as Emma and Clover arrived. 'This is our Emma and this here young lady is Clover.' A tall man, with thinning hair approached them; arm outstretched, ready for an impending arm shake.

'Hi, I'm Nick. Katie's son.'

There wasn't really any need for the introduction. Emma had heard plenty of stories about him from Katie. Mainly how successful he was; living in London, manager of a well-known National Bank. Still, Emma smiled and returned his handshake.

'Hello Clover,' he said, kneeling to speak to Clover on her level. 'I've heard so much about you. Katie really loved having you visit her. I love that you're also wearing her favourite colour.'

Clover smiled shyly at him. It wasn't like Clover to be shy; she was always quite confident and outspoken.

'Do you mind going into the church and helping Reverend John to set out the programs, while I talk to your mother for a minute?'

Emma looked a little confused as she watched Clover happily nod and follow the Vicar inside the church.

Nick shuffled his feet and cleared his throat, glancing around as if searching for the right words. People were slowly entering the church, but Emma's attention couldn't drift away from the man before her. She felt a sudden chill run down her spine, anticipating what was coming next.

'I hope you don't mind,' he began hesitantly, 'but there's something I need to talk to you about. You see, my mother had been talking about this ever since your arrival in the village; it has something to do with the close relationship between you and Clover.'

Emma watched him intently, her eyes narrowing with curiosity. Her heart raced in anticipation as Nick continued speaking.

'Mother had her will adjusted,' he said in a soft voice. 'She's decided to leave you her house. It may not be much, but it's yours now... she knew you'd need it more than I do. Plus, she wanted to give something special to Clover.'

At these words, Emma's breath caught in her throat. She could hardly believe what she was hearing. Before she could find appropriate words to reply, the Vicar emerged again from the church.

'Sorry to interrupt.' He said, walking over to them. 'But the service is due to start soon, the hearse will be here any minute.'

'No problem at all.' Nick replied for both. 'Emma and I will catch up after the funeral. I'll be staying for a couple of days too, to sort some paperwork out.'

Emma stood in stunned silence, unable to process the news she had just received. She let her body move mechanically, following Nick and the Vicar into the church. As they entered, Emma spotted Clover sitting alone in one of the front pews. The service was small and intimate, yet joyous and full of life. Emma watched as Clover sang along with all the hymns, dabbing at her eyes during readings that detailed Katie's life.

Afterwards, the small crowd made their way down to The Horse and Cart where a buffet had been set up for those who had travelled far for the funeral. As Emma reached out to take Clover's arm, intent on returning home straight away, Nick caught up with them and asked if they could talk at the wake.

Clover cut in before Emma could respond. 'What conversation?'

Emma slowed their steps until some distance had grown between them and the rest of the mourners. 'There's something I need to tell you, before you hear it from Nick,' she began tentatively.

But Clover smiled uncertainly. 'I already know. Katie left us her house.

Astonished, Emma stopped walking completely.

'When did she say this?'

'A long time ago, maybe before Christmas or maybe even before.' Confidence rising, Clover continued: 'So when are we moving in?'

Amused despite herself, Emma laughed incredulously. 'We're not! I'm telling Nick we can't take her house.'

'But we're not taking it, it's a gift.' Clover continued. 'Plus, we can live in it, when Grandma June comes to stay, because I don't want Grandma June sleeping in my bedroom.'

It was true, Emma thought, picking up her walking pace as they headed towards the Horse and Cart. She still hadn't figured out where her mother would be staying when she did come back to live with them. There definitely weren't enough rooms at Hope Cottage, and with her mother living back home, then surely, she could take up some of the care for Martha and James? Emma considered her choices as she pulled open the door to the Horse and Cart, rejoining the small crowd, who had already ordered their first drinks.

Eleven

4 years later.

Emma finished pressing Clover's new uniform, the steam from the iron filling the room with a warm, comforting smell. She hung the clothes up on the hangers balanced precariously on the doorframe, then moved to the kitchen. The smell of pancakes reminded her of Sunday mornings when she was a child and she smiled at the happy memories before giving the batter one last whisk to fully combine it.

'Breakfast's ready.' She shouted up the narrow staircase, which led off from the kitchen, listening intently for any movement upstairs. When no response came, Emma sighed and decided to go check on Clover herself. As she walked up the stairs, her eyes fell upon the pictures lining the wall. One in particular caught her eye; a photo of Katie standing outside their front door, surrounded by immaculately kept rose bushes in full bloom. It had been a gift from Nick four years ago and still filled them both with gratitude.

Reaching Clover's bedroom door, Emma knocked before entering, feeling blessed for all they'd been given.

Emma shook Clover's shoulder gently, letting out a soft sigh as the girl buried herself further in her duvet. The house was still chilly from the overnight chill brought by the early September morning, but the coal fire and aga oven were starting to warm it up.

'Clover!' Emma said, a little more firmly. 'Come on, if you don't get up now, you'll be late for your first day of high school.'

The covers moved and Emma caught a glimpse of her daughter's flaming auburn curls and slim frame. It seemed like only yesterday that they had been enrolling in primary school together.

'And if you don't hurry,' she added, playfully, 'I might just have to give Toby your pancakes.'

At the mention of his name, their Jack Russell puppy bounded into the room, his tail wagging eagerly.

'Alright, I'm coming, I'm coming.' Clover finally managed, pulling herself out of bed and wrapping her dressing gown around herself. Emma threw the curtains open, casting light across the small room. Gathering up the small pile of clothes on the floor, she followed Clover back downstairs.

'Are you nervous?' Emma asked, as they sat at the small table in the kitchen.

'Not really,' Clover replied quite confidently. 'I mean, I'm nervous because I've never been to the school before, right? But I've got Emily with me. And she's in my form group, so it's not like I'll be on my own.'

Emma smiled to herself. It was funny to think of the tiny little girl Clover was, and how she had turned into such a young confident lady.

'Well, your uniform is all set, so you just need to get ready. We told Emily we'd meet her at hers by 8.30pm and then you're walking up together.'

'Yeah, yeah, alright, I'll go get ready.'

Giving Toby, the scraggly mutt, the leftovers from their plates, Clover grabbed the clothes hanging from the door and dashed up the stairs two at a time, her school uniform wrinkled in her arms. Emma rolling her eyes at the wasted time she'd put into ironing them.

Gathering the strewn dishes of breakfast, Emma's thoughts were interrupted by her mother busting through the front door.

'Hello? Are you still here?'

Emma smiled to herself at her mother's typical words.

'No, we've gone.' Emma called out sarcastically, eliciting no response as she knew her mother wouldn't pick up on the subtlety of her joke.

'Oh good, I was worried you had left already.' June replied matter-of-factly despite its unnecessary nature. 'I wanted to see Clover before she went.'

'She just ran upstairs to get ready for school, so you're right on time.'

June picked up the teapot that had been sitting on the stove since breakfast, poured herself a cup of tea, and settled down at the small kitchen table. Emma couldn't help but reflect on how much life had changed in the four years since her mother moved back to their village. She had never anticipated that this move would be the best thing for all of them in the long run. With her mother removed from the toxic city environment and given a newfound purpose, her parents' house now felt full of life again - the garden flourished with hand-grown seasonal vegetables, Emma was able to continue her training career, and June stepped up to help care for Clover whenever she needed it. A special bond blossomed between June and Clover;

even though Clover hadn't known June for the first eight years of her life, she quickly grew to fill the gap that Katie had left behind. They spent their days shopping and going to the movies. James had taught Clover so much about growing vegetables, while Clover then taught June what James could no longer do.

'I'm taking Mum out into town today.' June announced, settling down at the small kitchen table. 'She said she wanted to go to the bakers and choose a cake for Clover, for later when she comes over. You can come if you want?'

'I'm meeting Claire for lunch later, to help drown our sorrows of our children growing up.' Emma joked, 'Will Grandad be, ok?'

'We will time it around his nap time, so he'll be perfectly fine. Plus, this afternoon the nurses are coming round to check on him, so that will help break the afternoon up.'

Hearing footsteps on the stairs and then Toby coming first at full speed, just about stopping before crashing into the wall, their conversation ended. Emma and June sat anxiously waiting to see Clover dressed for the first time in her new uniform. Emma only hoped that she hadn't creased her shirt in the short moment that she'd been in possession of them.

'Oh my, you look beautiful.' June gasped, as Clover came fully into view. 'So smart and grown up.'

Emma couldn't disagree. The new uniform was a step up to the casual primary school uniform which clover had worn for the last seven years of her life.

'You do look very smart.' Emma beamed. 'We'll get a picture before you leave, I made sure to get a film at the weekend.'

Taking a seat at the table, Clover handed Emma a hairbrush and hair band so she could finish her hair.

'Are you nervous?' June asked, 'When your mum started high school, she cried all morning not wanting to go.'

'I'm feeling a little nervous now my uniform is on, but at least I already know people that are going, and I'll be walking into school with Emily.' Clove reassured.

'You'll be absolutely fine, before you know it, you'll have your skirt rolled up as high as your knickers and sneaking cigarettes behind the bike shed.'

'No, she will not!' Emma chided, 'Mum, you can't go putting such ideas into her head.'

'Oh, they all do it.' June brushed off, 'There's no point denying it, I'm sure you did it too.'

'No, I did not!'

'Sure, she did.' June winked at Clover, which made her laugh and Emma couldn't help but notice that it did seem to settle her nerves.

'Right, come on you, shoe's on, we'll get a picture and I best get you over to Emily's house.'

Standing outside of their red front door, Emma couldn't help but remember the picture of Katie, who was stood exactly in the same spot. Wondering if Nick, too had a picture taken outside of the door on his first day of school.

'Right, time for me to go.' June announced, 'You have a great day, my lucky little Clover.'

Twelve

4 years later

Emma rummaged through her bag, the fabric tugging between her fingers as she felt for her mobile phone. The sound of a beep upon locating it made her pause - she was still getting used to this tiny device in her hand. *'NEW MESSAGE'* the pixelated screen displayed. Navigating the screen; using the keypad, one finger at a time, she found the message options.

Mum, Having GR8 time, C U L8TR, Clover x

'What's that?' Martha mumbled next to her, pointing her arthritic hand at the small device Emma held in her hand. Emma had tried time and time again to explain the use of a mobile phone, and how everyone had them. Unfortunately, at the age of 82, Emma doubts Martha will never understand. Since losing James a few years previously, due to another stroke, Martha's mental health has taken a steady decline.

'It's just a text message from Clover.' Emma began, until she was interrupted by Martha.

'Eh?'

'A text message Grandma, from Clover.' Emma tried again, but a little louder and slower. 'She said she's having a great time and will see us later.'

'Later?' Martha quizzed again, despite already discussing this just moments before.

'Yes, for her party remember. We're throwing her a sweet sixteen party in the village hall.'

Martha grunted, but luckily June came back into the room with a pot of tea and a plate of biscuits. Despite her previous years of being a carefree adult, Emma couldn't fault her mother now. In one way she looked up to her now. Since James's passing, she had really stepped up again into the caring role she's unfortunately had to take on.

'I've just had a message from Clover.' Emma repeated back to her mother. 'She said she's having a great time.'

'Oh, I am pleased. She was so excited to go on her own with her friends. Her own little independent party.'

As June poured the tea, under the watchful eye of Martha; ensuring that the milk was poured into the cups first, as not to damage the bone china. Emma couldn't help feeling emotional after sending Clover off into the main city with her friends and new boyfriend Max. She'd insisted she wanted a day out with them, before joining them in the evening for her main party.

'Where are they going first?' June asked, breaking Emma's thoughts.

'They went bowling this morning, I imagine they'll be having lunch now and then on to do some shopping, no doubt to get some new clothes and makeup for tonight.'

'Sounds perfect.' June sighed dreamily. 'I remember when I was sixteen. Me and my friend Jackie went into town and tried our hardest to find me a boyfriend. I was adamant I wasn't ending my sixteenth birthday without having a first kiss.'

'No, you never.' Emma spluttered, trying not to laugh at the stories of her mother being sixteen.

'We did to, I'll have you know. We had these bell bottom flare jeans on, with a skin-tight white t-shirt. Hair volumed to the max. We were adamant we were both going to find a boy that day.'

'Well, how did it go?' Emma continued, curious to know more about this side of her mother she'd knew heard before.

'Well, it was so hot, that by the time we got off the bus, we felt as sick as two dogs. We ended up hiding out in one of the local cafes, feeling sorry for ourselves and wondering how else we could possibly get home without feeling sick anymore. By the time we recovered, we decided to actually order some food. I chose an egg sandwich, and as I bit into it, the yolk splatted all over my white top. I was traumatised.' June continued. 'Jackie suggested we go into the toilets to try and clean it off, but I only ended up spreading it more. In the end, I demanded we go home and try again another day.'

'Oh, that's so funny and awful at the same time.' Emma tried not to laugh too much, knowing how awful it must have been for the sixteen-year-old girl.

'The story isn't finished yet.' June continued. 'So, there we were, sat at the bus stop waiting for the next one to turn up. This lad walks past, I'm talking James Dean style. Tight trousers, leather jacket, the quiff in the hair. Everything. And he sits next to us, lights up a cigarette. Offers us one, and says, *'You've got egg on your top.'* Well, I was so embarrassed. I didn't know what to say. Jackie was sat next to me; mouth open unable to speak.'

By now, Emma was fully engrossed in the story, she was completely unaware that Martha had fallen asleep in her chair, little snores escaping from her every few seconds.

'Go on, what happened next?'

'Well, he starts talking to us. Asking what we were doing in town, where we were from, where we were going. Before I know it, he's getting on the bus with us. He said he lived in the next village and had to go through Glen Peaks. I don't know if that was true, or he was just bored and filling his time. We got talking on the bus, Jackie had finally found her voice and explained about our failed mission for my sixteenth. Finally, the bus came to a stop, and we got off.' June's eyes seemed to become dreamier as she carried on. 'Just before we got off, he came running after us and demanded the bus driver to wait a minute. Of course, the route was never that busy, so it wasn't too much of an inconvenience. He jumped off the bus, stood right in front of me and kissed me right on the lips. *'Mission Complete.'* He grinned at me, before jumping on the bus and driving off.'

'My goodness!' Emma exclaimed, 'Who was he?'

'To this day, I still have no idea. We never saw him again, no matter how many times we got the bus into town. Never even got his name, I don't think we even gave him ours. Just some stranger in the night, as they would say.'

'How strange, I wonder if he's out there telling stories of two girls he met, one with egg on his top?' Emma joked.

'Oh, stop it, you!' June chided. 'Come on, we better get on with the sandwiches for tonight now that her majesty is asleep.'

The silence in the house was deafening, but as June covered up Martha, Emma noticed that a sense of calm had begun to fill the space that only chaos had occupied before. Sunlight streamed through windows and illuminated the hallway, where June had spent hours sanding down dressers and cabinets, preparing them for coats of paint. The furniture looked new, despite its age, and gave off a warm glow that made the whole house feel alive again.

As she took it all in, Emma realized that this was what June needed most: activity and purpose. She couldn't imagine how much work must have gone into bringing everything back to life like this, but it was clear that June had poured her heart into every inch of the house.

Thirteen

Clover climbed onto her bed, standing with her feet resting on the edge of the mattress in order to reach the full-length mirror. She examined her reflection and smiled, pleased with what she saw. She had treated herself to new blue jeans that hugged her curves exactly right and a pale blue silk vest top that showcased her slender frame. Her auburn hair hung loosely around her face, cascading down over her shoulders. Slipping on the charm bracelet presented to her by her mother, adorned with a small silver clover to replace one lost many years ago; Clover was ready for the night ahead.

'You look beautiful.' Max announced, as he lay underneath her on her bed. Looking down at him, she couldn't help but roll her eyes. Yet again he was on his phone, trying to beat his top score on the game Snake, all so he could show his mates later. Clover highly doubted that he'd noticed her at all.

'Here, you got a charger in here? Batteries nearly flat.' He announced, before returning to his game. Passing him the charger, Clover sat on the bed and fired off a text message to Emily.

U Ready?

The familiar beep of her phone alerted Clover that Emily had read the message and she waited anxiously for a reply. Staring into the hand-held mirror, she meticulously applied blush to her cheeks and lined her eyes with kohl before heading to her party. What started as an intimate gathering between close friends had quickly gained popularity among the students at school – invitations were sent out and accepted by all but two. Fifty guests were due to arrive tonight - an impressive turnout for a sweet sixteenth in such a quiet village.

'Why wouldn't they have come?' Grandma June had asked, when Clover had first announced her surprise as the RSVP's started to roll in. 'The only thing sixteen-year-olds want to do is go wild and party.'

Clover shrugged at this reply, and supposed June was correct. After all every teenager loved a good excuse to stay out late, party and snog whoever was up for it. She just hoped it didn't get too out of hand with only her mother, Grandma June and Claire helping supervise.

The beeping of her phone, announcing a new message had come through, brought Clover back to the present day.

Nearly there. Can't wait.

Emily replied, which meant Clover and Max should get a move on and head over to the hall.

'Come on you.' Clover said, throwing his jacket in his face.

'Oi!' Max shouted, 'You've just made me crash, and I was so close to beating that score.'

Clover grumbled to herself as she made her way out of her bedroom. She had been paired up with Max, the school's resident bad boy, by their 'friends'. He had a reputation on campus and girls fawned over him because of his stylishly tousled hair and leather jackets. Whereas Clover stood out in the crowd with her signature auburn locks, perfect makeup and ever-present popularity. At first everything was going well for them, but recently he seemed more interested in his phone than her.

Arriving at the village hall, Clover couldn't help but be taken aback by its transformation. She knew Grandma June had been behind it - she must have gone on countless shopping trips into the towns nearby to get all the decorations. On each wall hung giant pink banners that read 'Sweet 16' in golden lettering. Tables were laid out around the edges of the room, leaving enough space in between for people to dance. Each table was covered with white tablecloths and number '16' balloons sat firmly weighted down in the middle. A sprinkle of confetti shaped like the numbers 16 was thrown atop of each tablecloth. As soon as Grandma June saw Clover enter, she rushed over to greet her.

'Happy birthday!' She screeched, bringing her into a hug. 'You look beautiful. Stunning. Doesn't she Max?'

Max managed to pull himself away from his phone screen, 'Yes she does.' He grinned at her, the grin that originally used to melt her all over.

'Hello darling.' Emma greeted her, apron still on from sorting out the buffet table. 'Everyone will be arriving soon; I've left a table free for you to put presents on. We'll pack them all up and get them out of sight once everyone is here.'

Clover smiled, between them, her mum and Grandma had thought of every single detail.

Clover's heart swelled with joy as she watched her friends and family laugh and talk in the town hall. They had all come to celebrate her 16th birthday, filling the room with their energy and love. She grinned down at Max, who looked up from his phone occasionally to smile back at her. Even he managed to put aside his devices and join her friends on the dance floor.

The vibrant music changed to a gentle lull as they all sang out in chorus: 'Happy Birthday!' She blew out the candles on top of the cake made by her mum, feeling truly special.

Heading home after everyone had left and the hall been tidied away, Clover linked arms with her mum. She was overwhelmed by the thoughtfulness of the nights event so much that she couldn't find words to express it. Emma smiled at her daughter, feeling proud at how she was turning into such a confident young woman.

'I'm so lucky to have you.' Emma announced, making Clover smile and lean into her.

The village was sound asleep as they continued their small walk home. Everything seemed perfect.

'I think I'll finish it with Max.' She finally said, breaking the silence.

'Then he's not so lucky.' Emma laughed, in turn making Clover laugh along too. She didn't know why it was so funny, but they didn't stop laughing until the minute they opened the front door of their tiny cottage.

Boiling the kettle, Clover changed into her pyjamas, and together they sat. Reminiscing of memories of old times.

Fourteen

2 years later

Clover shuffled into the break room, sliding past the other workers as they slurped their coffees and talked about office gossip. She grabbed her lunch from the refrigerator and settled at a small round table near the window. Out of habit, she grabbed her phone from her bag and quickly scrolled through the various messages. Emily had sent invites to a night out for the weekend, her mother had texted to remind about tea with Grandma June that evening, and amidst all of them was one from Ben, her boyfriend of only two months.

Clover had just turned eighteen when she got the job at a bank in the next town, a stepping stone until she figured out what she wanted to do with her life. From nine to five, she worked in a tiny room processing cheques, earning enough to pay for driving lessons - no more relying on public transportation.

'Hello Love,' Margaret, one of the banking assistants entered the kitchen, to join her. 'You been busy today? The counter has been manic, with it being Monday. I'm glad to rest my feet for a bit.'

'Not too busy, I expect it will be once we receive the postal cheques this afternoon.' Clover replied. Margaret had been with the bank for 25 years. The week Clover had started to be precise; a big celebration was held with banners and cake to share out amongst the staff. As lovely as Margaret was, Clover couldn't help but feel that she didn't want to be here for the next 25 years. *'Just work there for a little while.'* Grandma June had told her, the last time she'd complained of being bored in her stuffy box room. *'Get the experience in a big company like that, and the worlds your oyster. You'll see Clover, Luck will find your way, it always does.'*

'Here, I heard there's some promotions going around.' Margaret interrupted her thoughts. 'You never know, one might be coming your way.'

Before Clover could reply, the notification sound from her phone alerted her attention. Picking her up phone, she saw it was a message from Ben.

Hey Honey, fancy going 4 drinks 2nite? Pub quiz on @ the Swan.

Clover replied with a definite yes. It would help make the beginning of the week seem a little more interesting. She reeled off a text message to Emily too, inviting her and her boyfriend, Jake along.

'I best be heading back; those cheques won't process themselves.' She said to Margaret, a little cheerier that just five minutes before. Secretly Clover wondered if it was wrong to set a countdown on her phone for clocking out time.

※※※

Clover finished her tea with her mum and Grandma June and darted up the stairs to get dressed. She began tugging on a pastel sundress when Ben's horn blared from outside, followed by a call from her mum downstairs to say he was here. Hurrying down, Clover opened the door to find him in his Peugeot 106 — a car he had received for his eighteenth birthday — with the bass of his modified speaker system reverberating through the air. After she climbed in, Ben told her about his day learning to be a mechanic at his father's garage. As they drove away, she thought wistfully that she could ask if they needed help in reception, but quickly dismissed it — an all-male workforce would never welcome her.

Pulling into the pub carpark, Clover saw Emily already waiting for her outside of the pub entrance. All alone, Clover knew that her boyfriend had yet again 'other arrangements.' It was very rare that he came along to any of their get togethers.

'Hey, you,' Clover greeted her, giving her a quick hug, before heading in together, where they found the rest of Ben's mates already sat at 'their' table; drinks in full flow.

Clover saw Mark's eyes light up with excitement as they approached the table. His voice swelled, as he said too loudly,

'Oi, Oi, lads, it's our night for winning. Lucky Clover is with us tonight, that Jackpot is ours!'

Ben jumped in to defend her. 'Shut it, Mark!' He said firmly.

The comment stung more than usual today; as she had grown older, Clover had grown to detest the people who believed her to be lucky... or a personal lucky charm for them.

'I'll go get some drinks.' She said quickly, interlocking arms with Emily so they could escape the lads and have a quick chat together. As they approached the bar, Clover noticed a strange woman sitting on a bar stool sipping her red wine. She was the only female in The Swan, which was usually filled with either middle-aged men drowning their sorrows or young people trying to win some cash on a Monday night. The bartender behind the counter asked them what they wanted, and Clover had to reel off her usual order as he wasn't a member of staff she recognized. The woman caught Clover looking at her and offered her a quick smile, which she returned before making her way back to the table with their drinks. As they took part in the quiz rounds, Clover couldn't help but feel like she was being watched every time she turned around. At one point, she saw the lady chatting to an unfamiliar man who disappeared just before Clover looked again.

※❦❧❦※

'I think we'll call half time here folks.' The quiz master shouted out amongst the crowd. 'Go grab yourself some drinks, and we'll calculate the scores for this half.'

'I'm just popping to the loo.' Clover announced, pushing her chair back, the legs scraping against the tiled floor.

Emily too stood up, heading over to the bar, 'I'll get a round in while you're gone.'

Clover hurried past the bar area, feeling relieved that the woman was no longer there. Pushing open the door to the restroom, she scanned her reflection. She quickly pulled out her plush lip gloss from her bag and applied it carefully. As she caught sight of herself in the mirror, Clover heard the door creak open behind her. Glancing over her shoulder, she saw the same woman from the bar enter the small room. The woman moved quickly, pulling out a creamy lipstick from her purse and swiping it on her lips with precision. Her beauty seemed to fill every corner of the bathroom and Clover couldn't look away.

'You come here often?' The woman asked.

'Most Monday's.' Clover replied shyly, 'It's erm, quiz night Mondays.'

'I gathered.' The stranger replied with a hint of laughter to her reply. 'I'm Carol, by the way.'

'Clover,' Clover replied, unsure as to why she would be giving out her name to a woman she had barely met.

'What a unique name.' She smiled back at her. 'You know, you could be a model with that face.'

Clover remained silent, unsure of what to say.

'And with that name, you could be a star. I'm pretty sure there's only one Clover. You wouldn't even need a surname. It'd be like Madonna.'

Clover merely offered a giggled of uncertainty back as a reply.

'No, I mean it. That hair, that face, that name. You could seriously give Cindy Crawford a run for her money.'

Clover who never took compliments well, muttered a 'thank you.' And was grateful when she heard the quiz master calling for contestants to begin the next half.

'I've gotta go.' Clover said. 'Nice talking to you.'

Pulling out a small card from her bag, Carol handed it to her.

'Look this is my business card. Have a think and call me, yeah?'

Clover took it, turning it over in her hand, she saw it bear the company name:

Headturners

A variety of contact methods for Carol were clearly displaced on the front. From her email address to fax number, as well as landline, phone number and company street address.

Slipping the card into her bag, it stayed there for the rest of the night. She never told anyone about it, as it burned a hole in her bag. It also stayed there for the rest of the week. Until precisely 11.06am on Friday. When Clover really was bored of the monotonous week and couldn't bear to face the same routine which faced her the following week, and the week after that. Pulling the card from her bag, she turned it over a few times, before deciding on emailing Carol.

Part 2.
29th February 2016

Fifteen

Rolling over onto her stomach, she rummaged under her pillow and retrieved her phone. It lit up as soon as she pressed the power button and unlocked by recognizing her face. Her Instagram had blown up in the few hours since she had fallen asleep - hundreds of comments, a long thread of unfettered praise and criticism, and several private messages. She clicked on the one from her mum first.

HAPPY BIRTHDAY MY DARLING. SEE YOU LATER. LOVE YOU!

Her phone buzzed with happy birthday messages as she scrolled through her Instagram feed. She could hear Rob jogging up the stairs, singing a cheerful rendition of 'Happy Birthday'. Smiling, she tapped out replies of thanks and love hearts to her friends and family, feeling an overwhelming wave of gratitude for their support.

'At last, the Birthday Queen is awake.' he announced, as he walked through the doorway, holding a tray.

Clover grinned and positioned herself, so she was sitting up in bed, propped up against the duck feather filled pillows. Rob placed the tray on her lap, as he finished serenading her with the Happy Birthday song.

'I've remembered your favourite. Well, your mum reminded me how to cook your favourite.'

'Thanks so much.' Clover grinned as she looked at the plates in front of her; a stack of pancakes covered in syrup, with a small bowl of mixed fruit and a side of apple juice. She loved that he'd taken the effort to remember this was the breakfast she had every morning of her birthday while growing up. It was these little moments that made her feel she'd got so lucky with marrying a man like Rob.

'You tuck in, and I'll be back in a minute.'

Before Clover had chance to even take a bite out of her pancakes, a cloud of flowers walked back through the door, from each of his hands, also hung a couple of gift bags, marked with Clover's favourite brands.

'For you,' Rob said as he held out one hand as far as he could without letting anything fall. 'For you,' he continued, as Clover took each bag he handed. 'And finally, all of these are for you.'

She smelled the flowers, taking in the essence of the mixture. It took her right back to her grandma's garden, where as a child, she'd sit amongst the flower beds picking the perfect flowers to hand out as gifts.

'Honestly, thank you so much, you really shouldn't have.' Clover smiled up again at Rob.

'You don't know what's in them yet,' He grinned back, looking at the bags of presents, 'I might have got you some Tesco value goods in there, then you wouldn't be so thankful.'

What Rob didn't understand, was that despite the facade which she had created over the last couple of years, and the images which the media portrayed her as, she was far from the materialistic person she was made out to be. Fair enough, she loved buying the big expensive brands, she could afford them, why not? but simple mornings of breakfasts, dog walks in the forest and chilling by the fire watching a film while stuffing her face with goodies, were her favourite times.

She opened the card first, cards were always her favourite things. She still had stacks of them from her childhood stored at her mum's house. Cards from Katie, Dale, and Harry. All wishing her happy birthdays, until they themselves no longer existed.

'To my beautiful and gorgeous wife' The card read inside, *'What a lucky man I am to have you in my life. Happy 32nd Birthday! All my Love, forever and always, Rob.'*

He took the card from her and stood it up on the bedside table. Clover would move it later and display all her cards in one place in the living room, where they'd stay for at least 2 weeks. Taking them down was always the hardest part.

Moving on to opening her presents, she was pleased to receive the latest perfume from her favourite brand, which hadn't been released yet. More charms for her charm bracelet, symbolising achievements from the previous year; an Eiffel tower for the time she attended the Model of the Year award ceremony in Paris. There was also a book charm for the book she'd released just a few months previously; Being Me - It isn't all about luck. She cringed slightly thinking about the book, it was something her PR Manager pushed for, she thought against it for a good couple of years, but he really insisted that it was what her fans wanted and needed after all their dedication. He persuaded her it was time to fight back against the bad press which only assumed she was where she was out of 'luck' and that was only because of her name. Some even went as far as to suggest Clover wasn't her real name, until they went and dug into her past, even finding copies of her birth certificates.

Finishing the rest of her presents; a couple of novels from her favourite authors, some bath gift sets and her favourite chocolates, she once again thanked Rob. Climbing into bed with her, he stole a bite of her pancakes.

'Excellent, if I must say so myself, it's almost as if your mother cooked them herself this morning.'

He grinned, waiting for his last sentence to kick in.

'She isn't?' Clover responded astounded, but before Rob had time to answer, Clover was flying down the stairs and heading straight towards the kitchen. He lay back, as he heard the squeals of delight coming from Clover, after realising the mother she hadn't seen for 6 months was indeed the one who had made her birthday pancakes. He decided to leave them for a while before heading down and joining them.

'You looking forward to tonight?' Her mother quizzed her, as she made them both a cup of tea.

'Yeah, it'll be great. Although to be honest, I think I'm getting a little old for these parties now. I'm more looking forward to the weekend away that Rob has booked me. Secluded, and away from all of this.' Clover replied, waving her hands in the air to stimulate the environment she was in.

'Too old, never!' Emma mocked, 'Don't let Grandma June hear you saying that! Talking Grandma June, she sends her apologises again for not coming today.'

'She really needn't apologise, I told her last time we spoke, I didn't expect her to make the journey and party away the night.'

'Well, you know what she's like, always the one for a good party, but she just really isn't up for it, no matter how young at heart she is.'

Clover couldn't help but feel her heart sink as she thought of June. Each time she visited, the years seemed to have taken a toll on her face, adding more wrinkles and greying strands of hair. Growing up, Clover had never seen June as a typical "grandmother" figure - she was more like an older best friend. But since Martha's passing, June had begun to take on that role. Clover had offered to pay for garden maintenance and a cleaner to come a few days a week, but in true independent-woman form, June had refused. The last time Clover visited, she noticed that all of June's belongings had been moved downstairs, indicating that she was now living only in the two main rooms.

'So, what are the plans for today?' Emma broke Clover's thoughts, bringing her back to the present.

'Well, I actually have no plans! I thought I'd chill out here, relax a bit before having to get ready.'

'Sounds perfect.' Emma replied, grinning while pulling out another bag from underneath the counter. 'I had a feeling we would be needing these.'

Pulling the bag towards her, Clover pulled out the contents and already knew this was the best way to start her birthday. The bag held; new pyjamas, face masks, chocolates and her favourite DVDs, her mum always insisted on saving.

'Brilliant.' Emma grinned back, 'Although, you do know, Pretty Woman and Dirty Dancing are all available on Netflix now, right?'

Sixteen

Clover's gaze swept across the majestic room, and she drew in a sharp breath of admiration. The event planner had transformed the already impressive venue into a scene from a fairytale. Bulb-shaped fairy lights intertwined with vintage banners hung suspended from the lofty ceiling, casting an enchanting warm light on the antique furniture below. Decorative mason jars filled with more tiny bulbs flickered atop rustic wooden slices scattered along each table, draped with elegant white lace tablecloths. The aroma of delicious cuisine wafted down the hall as the caterers busily prepared a mouth-watering buffet spread to serve her guests.

Rachel burst through the door, her voice piercing the silence as she exclaimed 'This is amaaaaaazing!' She sashayed across the room in towering four-inch heels, hips swaying with each step. Her legs seemed to go on forever, and when she threw her arms up to hug her friend, they reached almost to her armpits. 'OMG Clove, this is going to be amazeballs.'

Clover had met Rachel at a photoshoot a few years previously. Despite her highly annoying screeching when she was over excited, she wasn't as annoying as first thoughts would presume.

'First one here.' Clover greeted her, 'Although not like you to be late for a party.'

Being seven years younger than Clover, Rachel was still in the party years. Every day was a party for her.

'And that is why I'm going to head to the bar now!' Rachel laugh, walking away the clicking of heals following her. 'Get those drinks in before it gets too busy!'

Clover's heart fluttered as the bright lights of the venue lit up the night, and soon there was a steady stream of guests making their way in. Greetings were exchanged as air kisses flew around and presents were hastily handed to her. She searched the room for familiar faces, spotting old colleagues she hadn't spoken to in years. Her gaze settled on the celebrities whose images graced glossy magazine covers.

'I've just been talking to what's his name off the telly.' Her mother shouted loudly over the music to her. 'He's ever so lovely. I can't wait to tell June.'

Clover was tugged onto the dance floor by old friends, her mother chuckling as she watched from the sidelines. As song after song played, Clover was spun around in circles, dipped and twirled, grabbed from different angles each time she tried to escape. Heavy fatigue descended on her halfway through the night and she managed to slip away unnoticed. Scanning the crowd for Rob, her eyes settled on him chatting with Rachel at the bar and she weaved her way over.

'Hey gorgeous.' Rob slurred. He'd obviously been taking full advantage of the free bar Rob had insisted on having.

'He's soooooo funny.' Rachel screeched. 'Like sooooo funny.' Both him and Rachel burst into hysterical laughed and Clover felt that she was easily a good couple of hours too late for the joke.

'Can I have a water please.' She called to the barman.

'Water?' Rob spluttered. 'It's your birthday, you want something stronger than water.'

'Hey hey.' He shouted over to the barman. 'Put the water down and bring her a double gin and tonic.' Beside him, Rachel once again burst out laughing. Clover decided not to respond, instead she took her alcoholic drink and made her excuse to go and find her mother; where she'd leave the drink there and hope her mum at least had a bottle of water on her table.

She found her mum bobbing and swaying away to the music, a big grin on her face.

'Hello lovely.' She said as Clover reached the table, 'Are you having a lovely time?'

'Lovely, thanks mum.' Clover shouted over cheers which were happening from the dance floor. She glanced up to see a circle had been formed and some random dance off was happening in the middle.

'There was supposed to be a big Happy Birthday sing along an hour ago.' She continued and then glanced over to where Rob was slung over the bar making Rachel laugh some more. 'But I think it's slipped his mind; I hope you don't mind.'

'Oh, trust me, I don't mind at all.' Clover laughed back in reply. It would have been the last thing Clover would have wanted. All these people who she barely knew, and they barely knew her singing Happy Birthday to her.

'I reckon you've got some lovely presents over there.' Her mother gestured to the large table piled high with multi-coloured boxes and bags. Clover bit her lip, not wanting to appear ungrateful but having been to parties hosted by celebrities in the past and received presents from them herself, she knew what these packages contained. Likely products they had been given for free to promote or their own merchandise. Growing up as a celebrity often meant that one of your rooms acting more like a warehouse - company's just sending out gift boxes or samples for you to post about on social media. It was common for celebrities to give away some of the gifts they had gotten for free which is why she knew how it worked.

'We'll open them together tomorrow.' Clover smiled back at her mum. Glancing out at the crowd, which was still dancing, it was obvious that they all were now far too drunk to remember where the birthday girl was. To Clovers relief, she was sure she could wait the rest of the party out in peace with her mother. Luckily it hadn't seemed long before taxi's started to roll up outside and the receptionist kept interrupting the DJ to call out names of people with taxi's waiting. As the numbers dwindled down, so did the tables as the staff who had been hired by the event planners cleared them away one by one. Before she knew it, the only people left were Clover, her mum and Rob and Rachel; who were still drinking at the bar.

'I'm going to take mum up to her room.' Clover interrupted them at the bar. She hadn't seen Rob for most of the night, so it didn't faze her much as he waved her away and told her he'd be up to join her soon after they'd finished their drinks. Leaving them both still laughing together, Clover took her mum to the hotel room they'd booked at the venue, before finding her own room and collapsing into bed herself.

Seventeen

2 years later

'There must be something out there?' Clover demanded down the phone.

'Look Clove, I'll be honest with you here. Cards on the table type of talk.' Her Agent replied, and she could almost hear him rolling his eyes down the phone line. 'You don't have many years left doing what you're doing. The younger models are quickly coming in. You won't be the golden girl for much longer.'

'It's Clover. Not Clove.' Clover reprimanded. 'I'm not out to be a golden girl. But there must be something else?'

'The hair dye deal is a great deal. Clover.' He replied, ensuring to emphasize her name. 'Plus, it's a long contract. Age has no end when it comes to hair dye.'

'I don't even dye my hair!' Cover repeated in despair.

'Look, I need to go. Just think on it yeah. It's a great deal!'

Clover hung up the phone, her heart in her throat. She had never imagined that work would dwindle out and not come looking for her. She had never allowed herself to even think about what life would be like without the luxury of having endless opportunities at her fingertips. Laying back, she felt deflated and worried about what was next in stall for her. The ringing of her phone jarred her out of her thoughts.

'Yes?' Clover replied, a bit too abruptly, not looking at the number and jumping to assumptions that it was her agent with a better offer, when in reality it was her mother. The tingling down her spine told her something was wrong before it was even mentioned. 'Honey, its mum.'

'It's Grandma June.' Her mum continued. 'I think you should come.'

Hearing the crack in her mum's voice, Clover hung up the phone and without a second thought, she started packing her bags in preparation for her journey to Glen Peaks. She knew Rob was away on business so there was no stopping her; it felt like it was only a matter of minutes before she was sitting behind the wheel of her car, speeding down the open road. She relished in the feeling of freedom that came with being alone in a car, and as she crossed over the stone bridge and passed the sign which read 'Welcome to Glen Peaks', Clover couldn't help but feel a sense of coming home. The years melted away from her memory as she navigated the small roads with ease and familiarity. However, when she reached the village, Clover couldn't help but notice how much it had changed: where local stores used to be, now only empty shells remained as online shopping had taken over. She even noticed that the old post office had been converted into a quaint little cottage, although its name and original signage were still attached to its exterior wall.

The houses that used to belong to elderly residents who had passed away had been snatched up by young families looking for a bargain. Many of these houses still had their original windows and lacked central heating, making them all the more attractive to first-time buyers with an eye for potential. And everyone seemed to have two or more cars per family; no one worried about how far away the village was from amenities. Instead, they were pleased with the upgrades the village had seen and delighted in watching children running around outside, tossing sticks off bridges, and playing in the improved playground. Turning off her engine outside of her mother's cottage—which she still referred to as Katie's old house—she smiled to herself. Despite the new windows her mum had put in a few years earlier, it looked identical to the way it did when she left. She'd constantly offered to help her mum renovate or buy a larger house, but Emma always refused, saying that one house was enough for just her.

    Clover smiled as her mother opened the door to the cottage and walked out to greet her. It had been a good couple of months since they had last seen each other, and Clover couldn't help but think how much she had aged. Emma had been filling her in on June's condition over the last six months, however Clover couldn't help but feel that some things were hidden away.

'I got here as quickly as I could.' Clover said, running over to her mum and hugging her tight. The smell of lavender filled the air, making Clover want to hang on a bit longer. 'What's happened?'

'You better come inside, we'll have a cup of tea and I'll fill you in.'

Clover felt instant relief as they crossed the threshold and she saw the fireplace burning bright and inviting. She settled down on the sofa, warmed further by its heat, while Emma busied herself in the kitchen. A few moments later, she returned with a pot of hot tea and two teacups which she set down on a table in front of them. With a gentle smile, she began to explain.

'Just a few days ago, she really took a turn for the worse. I went up to the house to see her in the afternoon, as I normally do. The nurses had already been to make sure she'd had her medication and when I went in, I knew something was wrong straight away. I could just feel it in the air.' Emma continued, her voice full of emotion, Clover just knew it wasn't going to be nice to hear. 'I called out for her, but there was no reply. So, making my way through to the living room, I found her slumped in her chair. I tried shaking her and calling her but of course there was no response. I called for the ambulance, and they came as quick as they could. She's in the hospital now, but they've said she'll be lucky to last through the night, and I just knew I had to call you.'

'Oh my.' Was all Clover seemed to manage at first, before her mind went into overdrive. 'Did she come round? Did they say what had happened? Did you contact the nurses? When can we see her?'

'Firstly, we can only go during visiting times unless they call us beforehand, which now isn't until 4pm. She is conscious now, but very drowsy and isn't really making much sense, but she does spend more time asleep than awake. They're still unsure what has happened, they said it may be just purely her body losing its fight to the cancer and slowly shutting down. Finally, the nurses said she was sleepy when they went in to see her, but she took her tablets as normal, and her stats were all good then.'

Picking up her cup of tea, Clover somehow had lost the appetite for anything and gently placed it back down on the table. Soon it would just be her and her mother left out of the family. Even though June was late coming into their family at Hope Cottage, she fitted in like the missing piece of the puzzle they all never knew was missing. Even though Clover doesn't live in the village no more, life will still be very strange without June in it. The life and soul of every party, regardless of how old she got.

'I'll take my bag upstairs.' Clover suggested, standing up and wanting some time on her own. 'I'll try and call Rob too, to see if he got my message.'

'Doesn't he know you are here?'

'I left him a message, I tried to call earlier and he's just so busy at work, he can never answer calls no more. I keep telling him he really doesn't have to work so much, but he insists. I'm lucky if I see him most evenings now with the number of meetings he has on.'

Clover trudged up the stairs, carrying her bag that had been abandoned at the bottom. She was met with unfamiliarity when she opened the door to what used to be her childhood bedroom. The walls were no longer a light blue, but rather a deep purple, and all of her old furniture had been replaced with sewing machines, paint supplies, and wooden shelves overflowing with crafting materials. In the corner of the room was a single daybed, where Clover would be staying for the next couple of days.

Pulling her phone out of her bag, she sighed as she saw that Rob still hadn't responded to any of her messages or calls. He had told her before he left that his work meetings now required all phones to be turned off and that secretaries only took notes. *What kind of meeting could possibly require such a strict policy?* Clover thought as she dialled his number yet again to hear his voicemail message asking her to leave a message.

Frustrated, she tossed the phone onto the bed and decided to change into something more comfortable - here at Glen Peaks, she could wear clothes that weren't as formal as back home, where she always had to look her best in case the paparazzi snapped photos of her. She stripped down and put on a pair of leggings and an over-sized hoody, tying her hair up into a ponytail. As she did so, Clover felt like a weight had been lifted from her shoulders.

'We've got about an hour before we need to leave.' Emma shouted up the small stairs. 'Do you want a sandwich?'

'I'll be down in a min.' Clover shouted back, smiling to herself, as memories of her teenage years creeped in. Emma always seemed to be constantly shouting up the stairs for her, at one point in her life.

Eighteen

Clover drove to the hospital, her hands tight around the wheel as Emma's phone lit up with an unfamiliar number her face drained of colour. Gingerly, she answered, and a trembling voice came down the line. The conversation was mumbled and brief as Clover strained to hear what was being said. Tears filled Emma's eyes and she quietly said 'We're on the way now' before ending the call. She clutched her phone tightly in her hand and declared 'They've said its time.' In that moment, Clover reached over, put her hand over Emma's, and stayed like that until they reached the hospital.

Clover pulled into a space in the carpark, too consumed with nervousness and dread to bother with the parking meter. She kept pace with her mother as they marched through the winding hospital corridors, each step becoming heavier as they approached their destination. When they reached the entrance of the ward, Emma pressed the buzzer system impatiently as if it held the answers to all their questions. Even though only seconds passed, Clover felt like she'd been waiting an eternity for a response.

'Ward 106.' The crackly reply finally came.

'We're here to see June.' Emma replied, trying to keep her voice emotionless.

The buzzing of the intercom indicated that the door had been released. Before it had closed behind them, a nurse was already greeting them.

'This way please.' She directed them, into a room labelled 'Family waiting room.' Clover knew they were already too late. 'Someone will be with you in a minute.'

The nurse left them, in a room which was far too quiet. The sense of being in a library and being too afraid to talk washed over both. Either that, or the fear that if they spoke then they might crumble instead. Clover pulled out her phone, activating the screen, she saw that yet again there was no missed call or message from Rob.

Opening her message's, she fired off another one to Rob, continuing the thread of her unread messages.

Call me please. Xxx

The door opened and in walked two members of staff, one Clover presumed must have been a doctor and the other a nurse. They both took a seat opposite them and the look on their faces said it all.

'I'm so sorry.' The doctor began, 'We told her you were on your way, but she just couldn't hold on any longer.'

The nurse pushed a box of tissues across the table and directed them at Clover. Who was surprised, as she wasn't aware of the tears streaming down her face.

'Was she in pain?'

'No, she wasn't. The nurses who checked on her noticed a change in her stats, and that's when we called you. She was sleeping and we made sure she was comfortable.'

Clover offered a slight smile as a thank you. She was slowly running out of words.

'Would you like to see her?

'Yes please, that would be lovely.' Emma replied for them both.

They followed the nurse along the corridors, laughter coming from the rooms which led off it, as family and friends visited and tried to cheer up their loved ones. Finally, they came to a stop and were facing a closed door, the number 201 stared back at them.

'Ready?' the nurse asked.

They both looked at each other. The door was pushed open, and the nurse allowed them to enter the room first. A small gasp came from Emma as she saw her mother lying in the bed in front of them. Reaching her bedside, Clover couldn't help but notice how peaceful and beautiful she looked. Clover stood motionless; her gaze fixated on her grandmother. June lay in the hospital bed, her eyes closed and her skin pale and still. Clover's insides ached, knowing that she wouldn't feel the warmth of her grandmother's touch as she had always done when they hugged goodbye. Across the bed, Emma reached out to take June's hand in hers. The room was silent; all that could be heard were the occasional beeps from the monitors and whispers from the hallway outside. Even though tears brimmed in Emma's eyes, her lips remained pulled tight into a pained smile while she looked over at Clover. Disbelief seemed to hang in the air like a cloud.

'Shall we go?' she whispered to her.

Clover nodded back. The nurse seeing the exchange of communication escorted them outside into the corridor.

'What now?' Emma asked, suddenly feeling like she was able to talk.

'We'll do the formal paperwork here and she'll be taken down to the mortuary.' The nurse explained calmly. 'As soon as you've arranged the details with the funeral director, then they'll take over organising everything else.'

'The funeral director, right. I'll get on to it.'

Clover noticed the tell-tale signs - her mother's pursed lips and pressed eyebrows - indicating she was slipping into the familiar pattern of managing sadness with organization. Clover pulled out her phone from her bag, the vibrating alerting her to a call. Hoping that it was Rob returning her calls, she was disappointed to notice that it was her agent. Deciding she had better things to do at that moment instead of talking about hair dye, Clover cancelled the call and placed it back in her bag. An extra vibration alerted her that she had a message, *probably a voicemail* Clover thought to herself.

On the drive home, her phone rang again. Connecting to the Bluetooth settings in her car, she saw from the display that it was her agent again. Clover once again cancelled the call.

'Do you need to speak to him?' Emma asked curiously.

'Not today, I imagine he wants to know if I want to be the face of hair dye yet. I'll deal with him lat

Nineteen

'We've got to be at the funeral directors by 11pm.' Emma said as she scooped scrambled eggs onto Clover's plate. 'So, I thought I would take you out for lunch afterwards.'

Clover secretly smiled to herself, even with the advantage of owning cars, Emma still saw driving to the next town as a full day event. If they just went to the funeral directors and came back, they could be home within a couple of hours. It was almost written in stone that the trip needed to involve some sort of adventure, whether it be having lunch or browsing the shops; anything less than that was unacceptable.

'Sounds perfect.' Clover replied as she buttered her toast. 'Do we need to take anything with us?'

'Not this time I don't think. We should be good.'

Clover unlocked her phone and saw the notification that had just arrived. She still hadn't returned her agent's calls or listened to his voicemails, though days had passed since June's death. She remembered Rob calling late in the evening on the day of June's death; he'd mumbled his condolences and apologies. He said he was stuck in meetings all day and would miss her while she was away. Clover thought it was funny that he hadn't offered to come support her. Instead, she saw notifications indicating a spike of followers on her Instagram page - some follower had obviously shared her old photos, earning her new fans. She opened her contacts list and tapped on Rob's number, feeling certain that he wouldn't answer. The moment his voicemail kicked in, she hung up, opting instead to send him a message.

Going to the funeral directors today. Hope you're, ok? Miss you! Hopefully be back in the next couple of days. Xxx

'I think I'll go for a quick run before we head out.' Clover announced, standing up and clearing away her breakfast plates.

'That's fine, we've still got a good couple of hours, and I've got some bits to get on with.'

Clover pulled on her running shoes, securing her earbuds in place before heading out the door. Exercise wasn't her favourite pastime, but the fashion industry demanded she keep a certain figure. Over the years, she tried every sport imaginable from spinning to swimming, even taking dance classes and yoga. But it was volunteering for a charity run that made her realize her passion for pounding the pavement.

As she ran through the village, Clover couldn't help but remember long times gone. She still remembered which houses used to occupy old family friends. Imagining them tending to their flower gardens, or sweeping the foot paths. Crossing over the bridge leading out of town, Clover offered a smile to a man walking his dog. Though something about him seemed familiar, she couldn't quite place him.

Finally reaching home, Clover found her mum in the garden pruning Katies rose bush.

'Good run?' Emma asked, clipping some dead stems from the brush.

'Brilliant!' Clover replied, 'I'll just grab a shower and then I'll be ready to go.'

Clover stepped out of the shower, dried herself off and stared at her small pile of clothes she had brought with her. She bit her lip, unsure if she should dress formally or casually to attend a funeral director. Not knowing the protocol, she settled on a pair of black skinny jeans and an ivory blouse with lace detail. Her ears perked up and she quickly changed into the outfit when she heard her mother's voice downstairs. Straining to hear beyond the walls, there was no indication anyone had knocked on the front door.

'It's no problem at all.' A male voice echoed in the kitchen beneath her. 'It's the least we can do.'

Quickly getting dressed, Clover made her way downstairs to see who their visitor was.

'Ah, I think she's coming.' Emma announced her arrival, hearing her footsteps on the creaky stairs.

Leaning against their kitchen cupboards, a hot cup of tea in hands and looking totally relaxed, was the man she'd ran past on the bridge.

'Hi.' Clover greeted him.

'Clover, this is Ed.' Emma introduced them both, 'Ed, this is Clover.'

'I think I saw you earlier.' Ed smiled; his blue eyes sparkled as the morning light flooded through the kitchen window. 'I was walking Toms dog.'

'You did,' Clover grinned back a little shyly. She was suddenly acting like a schoolgirl, and she wasn't quite sure why.

'Ed is Nick's son. You know, Katies Nick.'

'Katies Nick?' Clover stuttered. 'Not the Nick from the funeral. And the house. This House?'

'The very one.' Ed replied for them.

'I didn't know he had a son?' Clover studied him further and was sure he couldn't be much older than her at all. Yet she had no memory of him being at the funeral, or Katie ever mentioning him.

'It's a long story.' Ed replied, spying Emma looking at her watch. 'One which I don't think we'll have time for now.'

'He's right Clove, we need to get going.' Emma interrupted. 'Sorry for kicking you out Ed, but we do need to get going.'

'No worries at all, I just popped by to drop off the flowers and card. Maybe I'll see you around Clover?'

'Oh, I don't know. I'm only going to be here for the next couple of days, and then I'll pop back for the funeral.'

'Well, you never know.' Ed smiled back, and Clover couldn't help wondering why he left her wanting to extend her stay. Sending the thoughts to the back of her mind, she quickly said her goodbyes, as she left their house and ended off to the funeral directors.

Twenty

Clover's phone jolted her awake, the blaring of its ringtone nearly shattering her eardrums. She blindly swiped at the screen and silenced it before allowing herself to open her eyes. Squinting against the morning light, she read the name which had flashed on her screen; her Agent, who had been relentless in his attempts for her to accept a hair dye modelling campaign. The thought of it made her stomach turn, but she didn't want to retire yet either.

Frustrated, Clover tossed the phone onto her bedside table and rolled over to try and get more sleep. But a different kind of worry started to bubble up inside of her as she remembered why she had gone to bed early; hoping for any type of response from Rob. She reached for the phone again, flicking through apps until finally coming to Instagram. There were still notifications she hadn't seen from earlier that day, but she cancelled them without looking closely and threw the phone back onto the nightstand. Pulling back the covers she joined her mother downstairs for breakfast.

'I'm going up to the house soon.' Her mum announced as she poured yet another cup from the teapot. 'I feel like we can't avoid it forever.'

'We're not avoiding it forever.' Clover protested, 'She's only been gone a few days.'

'Well, I need to go and find her some clothes to wear, so I might as well go up and at least clear out the food cupboards at the same time.'

Clover always admired her mother's 'get it done' attitude, while Clover would put off dealing with the house for a good while yet.

'When are you going?' Clover asked, feeling the need to go with her.

'Soon.' Her mother replied. A little too vague for Clover's liking.

'I'll go get ready then.' Clover had secretly hoped for a lazy morning, hoping to catch up on a Netflix series she had started weeks ago.

'You're like a teenager.' Emma chided her playfully. 'I'll tell you what, I'll go up and you can take a walk up there when you're ready. I'll probably be there a good couple of hours.'

'Are you sure?'

'Absolutely. You take your time and meet me up there. I reckon you don't get much time to do just nothing, eh?'

'Too right.' Clover grinned, taking her cup into the living room where she grabbed the remote and settled into the sofa as Emma busied herself getting ready.

It wasn't long before Clover herself was making her way through the village and heading up towards Hope Cottage. Noticing a shop, she hadn't noticed before, selling freshly baked goods, she decided it would be nice to grab her mum and herself a treat. Clover stepped into the small shop, her eyes grazing over the neat wooden shelves and wicker baskets. Her nose caught a whiff of the freshly-baked bread, and she admired the neat array of jams, pickles, preserves, and meats that filled the counters. Taking in her surroundings as she looked, Clover noticed some small details like jars of homemade honey with labels written in swirly handwriting and rustic signs declaring which type of bread was inside each basket.

Picking up a wicker shopping basket, she browsed what was on offer. Filling her basket with some multi-seed bread, a Bakewell tart, tomato chutney and some carnalised onion cheese, she made her way to the counter. There was a bell on the counter, with a note 'Ring for attention.' Clover thought it was quite trustworthy of the shop not to be manned while open, it certainly wouldn't be the case in the city. Waiting a few minutes before plucking up the courage, she pressed the bell.

'One minute.' A voice from the back called. Clover waited patiently, using it as an excuse to look around the shop once more. Back turned to the counter, she wasn't aware that the owner had appeared at the counter.

'Clover?' The voice asked, making her jump before turning around. 'Sorry.' He laughed. Standing behind the counter was Ed. His brown hair was slicked back, making his blue eyes stand out even more.

'Hi!' Clover said, placing her basket on the counter, and adding a packet of shortbread to it. 'Is this place yours?'

'It is.' He replied, running her purchases through the till. 'I've owned it for a couple of years now, there's also an online shop with bits being sold all over the UK.'

'That's amazing.' Clover replied, as she packed her goods into a brown paper bag. 'Mum or Grandma June never told me about this place.'

'I'm surprised, they were both regular people. They loved the Bakewell tart.' He grinned at her, taking the remaining product out of her bag.

Clover smiled back, handing over her debit card as payment.

'I tell you what, why don't we meet for a drink?' He asked, 'I can fill you in on everything before you head home.'

For some reason, Clover found herself blushing. She wasn't too sure what had come over her at all. Normally she oozed confidence.

'That would be lovely.' Clover finally found herself replying. 'I'm planning on going back the day after tomorrow. The funeral isn't for another week, and I need to go home and grab a few more bits.'

'Tonight then?'

'Tonight.' Clover grinned.

'Tonight, it is, I'll stop by at 7ish. Is that ok?'

'Perfect.' Clover continued grinning, as she exited the shop. 'See you then.'

The winding road to Hope Cottage gave only a slight pause in her journey as she glanced down at her phone. The bright screen illuminated yet another missed call from her agent but nothing from Rob. She carried on with an empty feeling in her chest.

Twenty-One

When Ed said he'd stop by at 7-ish, Clover imagined that he would be driving them somewhere. So when she opened the door followed by a gust of evening air which blew in. She found Ed stood on the doorstep, his dark hair tousled by the wind to find no car in sight, she was a bit perplexed.

'Ready?' he asked.

'Er, yeah. Let me just grab my bag.'

Heading back into the house, she quickly grabbed her bag and big her mother goodbye.

'Have fun.' Emma cheerily replied from the kitchen.

Heading back towards the waiting Ed who was admiring the rose bush in full bloom, he turned when he heard the door close.

'I've always loved this.' He said, 'I never got to see it until I came here. I've heard so many stories of its beauty throughout the years though!'

Clover smiled back at him. The rose bush seemed to be some form of legacy in the village. Everyone always remarked on it.

'Ready?' Clover asked, opening the garden gate for him to exit. 'Where are we going?'

'The Horse and Cart.' Ed pointed, right across the street, at the pub which sat merely a few meters away from the cottage.

'There?' Clover quizzed. 'Isn't that some old man pub?'

'It used to be.' Ed chuckled, 'Back in the 90's. It's lovely inside now.'

Clover eyed him suspiciously, not sure that The Horse and Cart could ever be lovely inside.

'Just wait and see.' Ed smiled back at her.

Clover stopped in her tracks as she stepped through the piercing oak door. Painted signs hung on the walls, inviting her into the space that had changed beyond recognition. Once two small and dark compartments, separated by a bar, now one large airy room had emerged from the dust of renovation. An old fireplace was now central to the design, creating an island of warm light while tables and chairs provided seating spaces around it. Exposed brick walls gleamed a sleek and polished grey in contrast with their previously chestnut shadowed panels and a new solid oak countertop enhanced the updated bar. The atmosphere was welcoming yet modern, familiar yet fresh.

'Wow, this is amazing.' Clover beamed, 'nothing at all like it I remember.'

'Yeah, it's pretty great now. The new owners took a gamble on it when it went to auction a good couple of years back.' Ed explained. 'They completely gutted it and spent what felt like years doing it up. The gamble paid off luckily, and this place is normally heaving at the weekends as people drive out for their Sunday lunches.'

Clover followed him over to the bar, where he ordered their drinks before guiding her to a table at the back of the room.

'So, tell me about yourself.' Clover suggested, as she took a sip of her drink. 'How did you end up in Glen Peaks? And more importantly, what's the big family story you said you'd tell me?'

Ed took a gulp of his cider, before setting it down on the table.

'Now, that is a story to tell.' He smirked, making Clover even more curious.

'Well, go on then. I don't remember Katie ever mentioning you.'

'That's because she didn't know of me.' Ed began. 'Let's just say, I was a pregnancy that never should have happened, with someone my dad never really knew.'

'Not a result of a one-night stand?' Clover gasped.

'I imagine that's what some people would call me.' Ed grinned to himself, knowing Clover hadn't meant anything malicious from her comment.

'Oh, I didn't mean that!' Clover chided him, 'It's just, after meeting Nick, I never would have said he was that type.'

'Well, he was young and carefree. Didn't have any cares in the world. Left my mother the next day without any hint of contact. She thought nothing of their brief encounter, and it wasn't until a few weeks later when the penny dropped, shall we say.'

'How did you she get in touch with Nick?'

'She didn't.' Ed continued. 'She raised me as a single parent, with the help of my grandparents.'

Clover couldn't help but think how similar their childhood lives were. Clover still didn't know who her father was.

'It wasn't until she passed after a very quick illness, around ten years ago, did I go on a hunt for Nick. It wasn't easy mind; she knew very little of him and only had his full name written on a scrap of paper with details of when and where they met.'

'How did you do it?' Clover quizzed him.

'The power of Facebook.' Ed grinned to himself. 'I literally flooded every known group or page linked to the very tiny details on the scrap of paper. I searched for every Nick or Nicholas Bould. Mum said she remembered him saying that he was two years older than her, so that narrowed it down slightly. The place they met, luckily had a 'down memory lane' page, which I was able to post questions on. Finally, someone came forward, saying they think they knew who he was.'

'And was it him?'

'It was. I sent him a message introducing myself and asking if he remembers meeting my mother. Luckily for me he did, however he expressed his sorrow that she had never called him back.'

'Never called him back?'

'Yep, apparently, he did leave his number on the pillow that morning. He only had to rush off as his mates were picking him up in the morning to bring him home. He said he waited and wished for weeks that she'd call, but she never did.'

'How bizarre. Didn't you say your mother said he didn't leave any contact details?'

'That's the story I was told yes, but who knows, maybe he did, and it fell to the floor as she got out of bed that morning or screwed up in the bedsheets. Maybe he didn't and he just doesn't want to admit he slept with a woman and left. Either way, I had to break the news that she'd passed and that I was his son.'

'How did he take it?' Clover urged, curious to know more of the story.

'He was silent. He went from replying to my messages instantly to nothing. Then a few days later, he gave his apologies, with some excuse of being tied up with work, but was happy to meet me. I went to visit him, the following week. I met his wife and the rest of his children; my stepbrothers and sisters to be precise. And the rest is history as they say. He told me about his mother; Katie and where he'd been raised. I just felt like I had to visit Glen Peaks, and here I am. I've never felt so at home.'

'That's definitely a story to tell.' Clover said, trying to drone out the vibrating from her phone which was happening on the table.

'It definitely is.' Ed said, 'You do know, I really wouldn't mind if you took that. Someone is obviously desperate to get in touch with you.'

Picking up her phone and turning it over, she noticed it was an unknown number. Five missed calls from an unknown number, with no voicemails. She declined it and turned her phone off. Secretly she was hoping it was Rob, finally having the time to talk.

'Nobody important.' Clover smiled, slipping her phone into her bag.

'So, you've heard my story. Tell me about yours.'

'My story?' Clover asked. Nobody asked her to tell her story, they all knew from years of being in front of the cameras and living in the public eye. Clover questioned to herself as to whether he knew who she was, or if he completely lived under the rock of Glen Peaks and knew nothing of the outside world.

'Your story.' Ed repeated, 'I'm not gonna lie. I know your status; everyone talks about you. The tourists come here to just try and get some of your luck. Did you know, they believe it runs through the river that goes right through the town? Hands down, I caught someone trying to swim in it last year.'

Clover couldn't help finding herself laughing at the ridiculousness of it. People really did do the stupidest of things.

'But they're not your story, are they? They are what they've read in the papers or what the media has made up. What's your story Clover.'

Clover found herself playing with the beer mats, twiddling them around in her hands to keep herself focused. Nobody had ever asked her that question before. Fair enough, she'd written her story many years before, but they had added more in to make it more dramatic. By the time it was finished, it wasn't Clovers story at all, just the story they thought the people wanted to hear.

'I'll be honest,' Clover began, 'There's not much to tell. I grew up here, with my mum and my grandparents. Katie and a few other residents became my best friends. And life just sort of planned itself out. I had no intention of being in the limelight. I didn't even know what I wanted to do with my life. I was scouted at a local pub quiz; they said I had potential. So, I went along to a casting and found myself the face of the top teenage makeup brand at the time. From there, I was contracted for more and more.'

'Well, that doesn't sound very lucky.' Ed grinned. 'Where's the magic fairies you used to dance with at the brook? Weren't you forced to drink tea made from crushed clovers as a child?'

'What?' Clover spluttered, nearly spitting her drink out all over the place. 'Surely people haven't said that?'

'The rumours I've heard are crazy!' Ed explained. 'I even had a woman come into the shop a couple of years ago. She was drafting a novel based on the witch that apparently cursed the town. She wasn't happy that I wasn't a local and couldn't tell her much at all.'

'She never was writing a book?' Clover quizzed again, baffled by his confessions.

'She said she was, I'm not sure how far she got.'

The conversation between them flowed naturally and time passed swiftly. Clover found Ed to be an easy companion, and he made her laugh like she hadn't in a long time. She was grateful for his understanding when it came to stories of Katie; Ed never once judged or belittled her memories of their past. In his presence, she felt like she could just be herself -- the girl that she had almost forgotten still existed within her. She wasn't a famous model, or an instagramer. She wasn't someone who needed to impress everyone around her. She was just Clover. Clover who she'd forgotten existed many years ago.

When the last orders bell rang out at the bar, they were both taken aback by how late it was.

'We better get a move on.' Ed said, finishing the last dregs of his drink.

Clover agreed, then ended up in a fit of giggles as she swayed and stumbled as she went to stand up.

'I think you've had a bit too much.' Ed laughed with her, as he supported her out of the bar and escorted her across the road to her front door.

'I've had a great time tonight.' Ed announced, 'We should definitely do it again.'

Clover fumbled with her keys, trying to position them into the yale lock on the door.

'I'm going home tomorrow.' She said finally sliding the key into the lock. 'Else I'd love to, but then I probably won't be back until the funeral and that'll be it.'

'We'll find another time.' Said Ed optimistically. 'Goodnight, Clover.'

'Goodnight, Ed.' Clover smiled, waving him off before shutting the door and collapsing down onto the sofa.

Twenty-Two

Clover squinted through the rain-splattered windscreen at the cars ahead of her. She had been sat on the motorway for almost an hour and the anxiety that had settled in her chest since leaving Glen Hopes hadn't dissipated yet. Her fingers drummed against her steering wheel as she once again checked her phone to see if Rob had replied to her message, which could have easily been lost in the torrential downpour pinging against the roof of the car. Streetlights blurred by in a seemingly endless procession as she drove home - her grip tightening with each red light that stopped her progress. A lump formed in her throat as disappointment at his lack of communication slowly crept in.

'Great!' Clover shouted aloud to herself, hitting the steering wheel.

An announcement blared from the radio, informing her that the motorway she was on was closed due to an accident. She glanced around and noticed other cars had come to a standstill, their engines shut off. She couldn't help but feel slightly jealous of the couple next to her, who had each other to share their frustrations with. Her phone beeped in its holder, alerting her to a notification. Reaching for it, she expected a message from Rob, but instead, Ed's name lit up the screen.

Hope you're not feeling too rough today! Have a safe journey!

Clover smiled slightly to herself, she'd barely met the man, yet she enjoyed his company more last night than she had with Rob for ages.

Currently stuck in traffic!!! Been a nightmare journey and nowhere near home. Enjoyed last night, Thanks x.

Clover replied and then instantly went to her inbox with Rob. The lack of replies from him was really upsetting. Making a mental note that she should talk to him about it over tea tonight, she was interrupted by Ed's instant reply.

Sounds awful! Nice and sunny here. Actually, I'm sure I've just seen some other weirdo in the river outside 😊. Definitely need to do drinks again!

Clover giggled to herself and before she knew it, she was pressing the video call button for Ed and placing the phone back in the holder. Surprised, he answered it straight away.

    'Hey!' he said, smiling at her through her screen.

    'I am soooo bored!' she replied, doing her best sulky impression.

    'I reckon you should have stayed here for a bit longer. Seriously it's bright and sunny. Look.'

    He turned his camera around, and she could see the sun blaring through his shop window.

    'Looks delightful! Maybe I should have gone in for a dip in the river to renew my luck before I left.' Clover joked; hearing Ed laugh at the end. She enjoyed making him laugh. Whenever she tried to joke with Rob, he often just rolled his eyes at her.

    'Talking of luck, I've been trying to hunt down that woman who wrote the book.'

    'Oh yeah. Any luck?'

    'I think I may have found the book, I'm not sure if it's her one, but there's definitely one listed on Amazon.'

    'On Amazon?' Cloved spoke curiously, 'So it was actually published then?'

    'Self-published, I believe, by the looks of it.' Ed explained, 'In fact, I might buy a load of them and sell them to the crazies who come in the shop. Actually, I'm thinking of changing the shop name, to 'The Lucky Clover.' I reckon I'll be rolling in it before long.'

    'Oh, shut up,' Clover laughed. 'I think today proves that I'm not as lucky as people make out. If I was, then surely, I'd be home by now, instead of being sat in miles of standstill traffic.'

Clover watched the screen, as Ed put his phone face up on the counter and listened as he served a customer.

'Sorry about that.' He announced his arrival back, his face filling the screen once again.

'Tell me more about this author.' Clover asked. Intrigued by the woman who had spent her time working on a story about her and Glen Hopes.

'I haven't found out anything about her.' Ed confessed. 'Her name is Gail Riley, but I can't find any social media accounts for her, and she doesn't seem to have written any other books.'

Clover rolled her eyes and shook her head, 'Someone who has been obsessing over some dumb luck story,' she mumbled.

He beamed at her response and continued, 'I think it's great. Just think, it'll be something to tell your grandkids when they're older.' Clover didn't respond, but out the corner of her eye she saw that the traffic was finally starting to move and sighed in relief.

'I think we're moving again. I'll have to go.' She told Ed. 'Speak soon yeah?'

'Yeah of course. Hope you get home quickly. Speak soon!'

'Bye.' Clover finally said, ending the call and joining the queue of slow-moving traffic. Clover squinted through the rain pelting her windscreen, struggling to make out the road ahead. A few cars had suddenly taken off and she watched as the speedometer of her car began to climb. Eager to take advantage of this small window of opportunity, she moved over into the right-hand lane, not noticing the car in her blind spot until its horn beeped aggressively. The sound of metal crunching against metal filled her ears and then the car was spinning wildly out of control on the slippery roads. There was one more crash before the car flipped and hit a barrier in the centre of the motorway. Inflatable airbags rushed towards Clover's face as all went still and silent, save for the cars that continued to rush past outside with no regard for what had just happened. She lay there helpless, hoping someone would stop and come to her aid.

'Somebody call for help.' She heard a male voice shout faintly amongst the noise of the traffic and rain. His face appeared at the smashed window.

'You alright love?' He asked.

Clover could only nod in response, feeling the tears stream down her face as another man appeared behind him. She heard the new man say something about calling for emergency services and felt her heart racing in her chest.

'What's your name love?' The man at her window inquired, his voice warm and inviting.

'Clover,' she managed to croak out before feeling a wave of exhaustion wash over her. Her vision blurred and she noticed a single raindrop slide from his hair, slipping slowly down his forehead until it fell off his nose.

'Clover, eh? That's a pretty name. I tell you what, why don't you tell me a bit more about yourself while we wait for this ambulance to arrive?' he gently encouraged her, but Clover could feel herself gradually succumbing to the heavy lids of sleep. She strained with all her might to keep them open, wanting desperately to answer his kind questions, yet a deep exhaustion has already settled in her bones. The man's voice faded in and out as Clover began to drift away—a final image of him looking calmly at her as if he knew exactly what she was feeling playing on the back of eyelids before they slammed shut.

Twenty-Three

'Clover, can you hear me?' a distant voice echoed in the darkness.

'Her stats are stable.' The voice said aloud. 'Somebody keep an eye on her, and we'll try and find some contact details. Get her cleaned up too.'

Clover tried to focus her attention on her surroundings, desperate to be anywhere but in the oppressive darkness. In the distance, she could hear a faint beeping noise and then the sound of heavy footsteps slowly drawing closer. She held her breath, listening intently.

'You know who it is, don't you?' she heard a female voice whisper close by.

Muffled voices sounded from a distance, becoming clearer as they came closer. Then the unique aroma of antiseptic and disinfectant hung in the air like a haze, signalling that Clover was in a hospital. In her disoriented state she felt someone take her hand, gently rubbing each finger and up along her arm before patting it dry with a soft towel. This process was repeated on the other arm. When the cloth moved to wipe sweat off of Clover's forehead, she fought to open her mouth, but her lips were so dry that she feared they would crack apart if she tried to speak. As the cloth was taken away, she concentrated on slow breaths to bring calmness back to her body.

'We've managed to track down her mother.' A voice in the distance said. 'She said she's on her way now.'

'Mum.' Clover whispered, although she didn't know if the words actually made a sound. The room had gone quiet again, so she tried again, but a bit louder. 'Mum.'

'Clover, can you hear me?' the male voice said, a rough hand, held hers. 'Clover, if you can hear me, can you squeeze my hand.'

She felt weak but managed to squeeze it as much as she could.

'That's great, Clover.' The man sounded relieved, and Clover was sure she can almost hear him smiling. 'I'm Doctor Ryan. You're in the hospital after having a road accident on the motorway.'

The faint memories came crashing through her brain, as Clover remembered the rain, the sound of metal on metal and the sensation of being spun around. She squeezed the doctor's hand tighter for comfort.

'It's ok, Clover, you're doing great.' He reassured, noticing her tighter grip. 'I want to see if you can try and open your eyes for me. Do you think you can do that?'

Clover cautiously opened her eyes, blinking in rapid succession as the harsh floodlights threatened to blind her. Squinting, she saw Dr Ryan's face in front of her; he was younger than the image her brain had concocted up, but his kind and careworn expression matched the comfort of his voice. She slowly lowered her arm from where it had been shielding her face.

'Hello there Clover.' He smiled down at her. 'Nice to see you.'

Clover smiled weakly, even though her lips felt like they're about to crack.

'We'll just raise the bed, so you're sitting a bit more upright, then we'll get you some water, shall we?'

Clover nodded, and watched, as he pressed the controls on the bed to make the back rise. A nurse came around to her other side, with some extra pillows and helped to support her as they were arranged around her. Another nurse had a small glass of water ready to hand her, a plastic straw stuck out of the top. Once in a comfortable position, the nurse eased the straw through Clovers lips for her, as she gently sucked the water. It's ice coldness hit the back of her throat, and Clover felt instant relief. After she had finished, Doctor Ryan performed some basic tests to check her reflexes.

'Can you tell me what you remember?' He finally asked, taking his position at the end of her bed.

'It was raining.' Clover began, 'and I'd been stuck in traffic for what seemed like forever. I just wanted to get home, so pulled into the fast lane and hit another car. I remember the car spinning so fast and I couldn't control it.'

Clovers eyes began to well up, as her voice started to crack. 'Are the other drivers, ok?'

Doctor Ryan offered a sympathetic smile. 'They're all fine, luckily.'

'On the other hand,' He continued, picking up a clip board. 'I reckon I should give you a rundown of your injuries.'

Clover eyed him worryingly and watched as he read the notes on his clipboard.

'Luckily, there's no broken bones. There's a lot of soft tissue damage, especially around the neck and bruising along the abdomen where the seat belt caused pressure. All scans have come back clear with no internal bleeding or injuries. Vital stats are looking great, but I'd like to keep you in overnight just to make sure everything is as it looks in paper.'

'I don't feel any pain?' She mentioned.

'That's because we hooked you up on our strongest pain relief the minute you got here.' He smiled back at her. 'Oh, and we got in touch with your mother, she said she'll make her way up as soon as she can.'

Standing up, Doctor Ryan placed his clipboard in the holder at the end of her bed. 'I've got some other patients to see, but the nurses will be in and out to make sure you've got everything you need.'

'Thank you. Really, thank you so much for everything.' Clover managed to smile back at him, as he bid her farewell and left her room. She placed her head back onto her pillow and closed her eyes briefly. Before she knew it, she was drifting off back to sleep, the pain killers keeping the numbness at bay.

Twenty-Four

Clover stood in the hospital bathroom, her face drawn and pale. She leaned close to the mirror, studying the deep purple bruise beginning to appear along her left cheekbone. Her stomach ached as she pulled up her t-shirt, revealing a multi-hued spread of blues, greens and yellows that had not been there just 24 hours earlier. Gently, she ran a hand over them, wincing at the tenderness. She was grateful for the loose-fitting leggings her mother had brought her.

'Clover.' Her mother's voice came through the door. 'The Doctor is here.'

'Coming.' Clover replied, readjusting her clothes, and running her mother's brush through her hair.

'Lovely to see you up and about.' Doctor Ryan smiled, as she entered back into the room. 'Looking at your notes, you slept well and had a bit of breakfast this morning too. How are you feeling?'

'Sore.' Clover offered a weak smile, as she sat down on the bed. 'My neck hurts to turn. Almost like I've slept funny.'

'That will be the whiplash.' Doctor Ryan confirmed. 'I can prescribe some painkillers for the pain to take with you. I'm happy with everything, so if you're happy, then I'm happy to discharge you.'

'That would be great.' Clover smiled, she still needed to find a way to get her car and belongings back.

'That's super. I tell you what, you finish off here, I'll go sign the discharge papers and come back with that prescription.'

'Well, that's good news.' Emma smiled warmly at Clover as she folded the neatly pressed clothes, she had brought her the day before and placed them into a bag. "Have you heard from Rob?" Clover asked nervously, fidgeting with the hem of her shirt. Her phone was still missing, and she had tried to call him yesterday from her mother's phone, but his phone went straight to voicemail. She'd left a message too.

Emma slowly pulled her phone out of her pocket, letting out a resigned sigh as it lit up and showed no messages.

'Not yet.'

Clover gave a weak half-smile at the sight, her stomach churning with anxiety - he had been expecting Clover back home days ago, yet he had sign or news of her whereabouts. With each passing moment, her worries grew more intense.

'I bet once we find your phone, they'll be loads of missed calls from him.' Emma reassured, finishing off packing her bag.

It didn't seem long before Doctor Ryan was back, with a small paper bag of tablets and her discharge notes.

'You're all set to go,' He smiled. 'I've arranged for Nurse Sally to take you out a back entrance. Your mother can go ahead of you to grab the car and meet us round there.'

'The back entrance?'

'Yes. Unfortunately, there's quite a few journalists waiting out the front.'

Clover hadn't even turned the TV on, while she was in the hospital. No papers had been delivered, and without her phone, she had received no updates on what was happening in the outside world.

'How did they know I was here?' She questioned, following them both out of the room.

'We're not sure. But they turned up, not long after you did, trying to find out what was happening. I imagine someone at the scene of the accident may have informed them.'

Clover's heart sank as she realized that if her accident had been broadcasted, then there was no way Rob hadn't heard. A chill ran down her spine as she thought of the possibilities: was he planning something? Did he even know or care where she was? She felt a knot in her stomach start to grow.

Making their way through the maze of hospital corridors she had to stop to catch her breath.

'Not far now.' Her mother reassured, and Clover couldn't wait to finally sit down in the car to rest.

Twenty-Five

Clover's grip on the side of the passenger seat tightened as her mother navigated the winding roads of Glen Peaks. Each bump sent a sharp jolt of pain radiating down her neck, a reminder of the accident that had left her stiff and bruised. By the time they had pulled up in front of her mother's cottage, her muscles were burning with exhaustion. She stumbled out of the car and into the front door with a relieved sigh, sinking into the welcoming cushions of the sofa. Guilt tugged at her as she forced herself back onto her feet, ignoring her body's plea to stay put but instead help her mother.

'What are you doing?' Emma asked, as she placed Clovers small bag at the bottom of the stairs.

'Making us a cup of tea.'

'No, you are not.' Emma Chided. 'You go and sit yourself down. I'll get that sorted for you in just a minute.'

Clover rolled her eyes; she knew there was no point in arguing. Taking herself back to the sofa, she pulled out the tablets the Doctor had given her. Piercing the foil sleeve, she swallowed back the allowed dosage. Leaning back into the cushions, she closed her eyes. Just five minutes, she thought to herself, then she'd try and deal with whatever she sensed was brewing. Feeling the heat of the fire, which her mother had just lit, made her feel drowsier. Her eyes were so heavy, that with all her willpower, she just couldn't manage to open them. Even when she heard the hushed voices in the distance.

'She's sleeping.' Her mother whispered. 'I'll tell her you popped by.'

Hearing the door shut softly and silence descend over the house, Clover's sleep deepened. She finally woke when her mother gently rose her, with a bowl of chicken soup.

'I've not got the flu.' Clover smiled weakly, remembering the times Martha would feed her with chicken soup if she was ever off ill as a child.

'No, you haven't.' Her mother smiled back, 'but it's full of good stuff which will still make you feel better.'

Pushing herself up into a seating position, Clover took the tray from her mother. Looking around, she noticed a few bunches of flowers which had been delivered while she was sleeping.

'These are from George,' Her mum pointed out, 'And those are from Jane, she lives just a few doors down.'

Clover smiled, as she took her first spoonful of soup. She couldn't deny that it made her feel better and was without a doubt better than the food she had had to endure at the hospital.

Another knock on the door broke the silence of the house. 'This must be more flowers.' Her mother stood, heading towards the door. Clover turned to see who it was as a giant bunch of flowers entered the room first. A smiley Ed peeked out from behind them, his eyes twinkled as he flashed a sheepish grin.

'Hey you.'

'Hey.' She smiled back, placing her tray down on the table in front of her.

'Oh, don't stop eating because I'm here. I've just come to drop these off.'

Emma took the flowers from him, no doubt having to find another makeshift vase to put them into.

'Please, take a seat.' Emma invited him in, 'you're the first visitor she's had today, where she's actually been awake.'

'Privileged.' Ed winked at her, seeing Clover's cheeks blush out of embarrassment. 'So, how you are feeling?'

'Oh, just a little sore here and there.' Clover glossed over just how sore she was and tried not to wince as she leaned over to grab her drank from the table.

'I did try and send you a message and call over the last couple of days, but your mum said you still haven't got you phone back.'

'Yeah, I still really need to sort that out. I take it everything will be with my car, wherever that is. I'll have to have look on google later to see if I can find out where everything might be.'

'Leave that to me.' Ed grinned, 'I've got a mate who works in the police, I'll give him a call and get some numbers for you.'

'Oh, you don't have to do that, really. I'm happy to sort it out myself.'

'It's no problem at all. You rest, and I'll see what I can find out.'

'Would you like a cup of tea, Ed?' Emma interrupted, shouting from the kitchen.

'Would love one, thanks.' Ed shouted back, then turned his attention to Clover 'As long as you don't mind me staying?'

'It's no problem at all.' Clover replied, knowing that him being there was helping to take her mind off the pain she was in.

'Well in that case.' He replied as he grabbed his bag, and pulled out a wrapped present. 'I've also got you this.'

'You didn't have to.' Clove smiles, 'Really, the flowers were enough.'

'I'd brought this before the accident, so not really a get well present.'

Clover looked down at the small, rectangular box in her hands and paused for a moment. She let out a quiet breath, and gradually peeled away the wrapping paper with delicate fingers. As the bright gold cover was revealed, Clover gasped—tiny emerald green clovers were embossed into the fabric. The title of the book glittered in intricate golden script: 'Fortune, Fate and Destiny; the tale of England's own lucky Clover'. And there, nestled in the bottom corner, was the author's name—Gail Riley.

'Oh my god.' Clover exclaimed, 'You found it. I'm not sure what the Fortune, Fate or Destiny is, but I'm sure to find out.'

'Well, I couldn't find it and not buy it. I got my own copy too.' Ed grinned back at her.

Emma bustled into the room; a silver tray balanced precariously in her hands. On it were three teacups, their handles lined up with precision, alongside a plate of crumbly biscuits.

'I've just had Claire on the phone, from work,' she said as she doled out the cups, an eyebrow raised in inquiry. 'They asked if I can go in and cover a shift tonight – do you mind?'

Clover shifted on the couch and winced slightly. 'Of course not, Mum. Honestly, I'm fine, just a little bruised, that's all.'

Emma studied her intently for a moment before turning back to the tray, rearranging each cup and saucer with great care. 'Are you sure? I can make some food for you before I go so you don't have to worry about anything.'

'I tell you what.' Ed interrupted them both, 'I've got no plans for the rest of the night, how about I grab me and Clover a takeaway, and I'll stay, and we can have a film night together?'

Clover smiled, secretly she would love nothing more, however she doubted she would be able to stay awake for much longer, let alone a film night.

'That would be lovely.' She found herself replying.

'That's sorted then.' Ed grinned back at her before turning to Emma 'You get yourself off to work, and I'll make sure everything is fine here.'

'I'll go get ready then.' Emma replied, a sly smirk across her face, as she exited the room.

'I just need to go change out of my clothes.' Ed said indicating to his work clothes which were still covered in bits of dry dough and flour, 'You'll be ok for 20 minutes, won't you? I'll grab the takeaway menus too!'

'Of course, I'll choose a film while you're gone. Any preferences?'

Ed shrugged on his coat and adjusted the collar. 'No chick flicks,' he said with a grin.

'Pretty Woman is out of the window then?'

'Yes, and The Bodyguard!'

'Great. I'll see what else I can find. We are not watching Star Wars though!'

He paused at the door and gave a mock salute. 'May the force be with you,' he said before slipping out into the night.

Clover managed a faint smile as she slowly made her way to standing. She winced in pain from her stiff muscles, biting her lip as she shuffled towards the sink to remove the dirty dishes that surrounded the living room. She limped over to the mirror, and surveyed her reflection. Her once meticulously tied bun had become dishevelled from her time at the hospital, and she unravelled it before brushing through the knots of her auburn hair, leaving it cascading down her shoulders. The fading light of dusk revealed the varying shades of blue and purple on her face that were becoming more prominent. Not wanting pity, she opted not to do anything else about them; instead, she lit the log burner and a few candles for some warmth, before curling up with Ed's book on the sofa. With each word she read, her eyelids grew heavier until finally they closed, and sleep wrapped around Clover like a blanket.

Twenty-Six

Clover hadn't heard her mother leave for work; she also hadn't heard Ed come back to sit with her. She was only woken by the sound of knocking on the door and then the smell of food. Prising her eyes open, she looked around slowly. The log burner was still burning, yet she was now also covered with one of Martha's crocheted blankets.

'And she awakes.' Clover heard from behind her, as Ed came over and placed a variety of clear plastic containers down on the coffee table. 'I hope you don't mind; I was starving so just ordered a selection from the local Chinese.'

'Local Chinese?' Clover quizzed; she wasn't aware of any takeaways in the village.

'Local as in, the only one that delivers to the village. 'For an extortionate delivery charge.'

Clover winced in pain, as she pushed herself up to position herself so that she could see which food he'd ordered.

'Hey, you ok?' Ed asked worried. 'Just tell me what you want, and I'll get it.'

'I'm fine, really.' Clover reassured, 'The stiffness of sitting still doesn't help, I think moving every now and again is the key. Let me just go grab some painkillers.'

'Tell me where they are, I'll grab them. You get that film started. Anything else you need?'

'Just some water please.' Clover smiled up at him, as he went into the kitchen. Reaching over for the remote, she turned on Netflix, thankful that she had forced her mother to buy a smart tv.

By the time Ed had got back, she already had the film picked out. It was the first on the suggested for you page, and one she had wanted to see for ages.

'Spiderman?' Ed exclaimed, as he settled down next to her handing her the tablets and glass of water. 'I wouldn't take you for a marvel fan.'

'Any hunky man, who enjoys rescuing people is fine by me.' Clover grinned; she'd noticed Ed had brought himself a cider. She would have loved to have joined him with a drink, but the tablets the doctors had given her had strict instructions of having no alcohol with them.

'Press play then. Also, we've got Chow Mein, Chicken Sweet and Sour or beef in black bean sauce.' Ed replied, leaning forward to grab the dishes.

'Chow Mein please.'

'Oh, and before we start, I spoke to my mate in the police. He said he'll have a dig around and find out what compound your car is at and will get back to me tomorrow.'

'That's great. Really, thanks a lot.'

Pressing play on the film, Clover settled into her seat. The painkillers had taken effect and a sense of contentment washed over her. She couldn't remember the last time Rob had spent an evening like this with her. Takeaways weren't part of her past lifestyle, and Rob was always too busy to watch movies with her. Ed caught her attention as she took a bite of food, smiling softly at her. She smiled back and returned to eating.

Not long into the movie, she noticed that Ed's breathing had slowed down and had become more relaxed. Looking over, she saw that he had fallen asleep. In the light from the TV and fireplace, she couldn't help but notice how strikingly handsome he was. Watching him sleep felt almost like an invasion of privacy, but she couldn't look away. A small scar on his chin caught her eye, and she wondered about the history of it. For now, though, all she could do was cover him with a blanket they could share. Clover tried to stay focused on the film, but soon found herself nodding off as well. Her breathing matched Ed's calm rhythm perfectly as they drifted off to sleep together.

When Clover woke the next morning, she found the space where Ed was empty. Sitting up too quickly, and her body being empty of painkillers overnight, she couldn't help but gasp as the pain in her neck shot through her. Emma appeared at the kitchen door, and

Clover glanced at her watch. It was 8.30am, probably the longest she'd slept since she was a teenager.

'He had to go and open the shop.' Emma smiled at her. A smile which showed her mother thought something more sinister was happening than what really was. 'Shall I grab you your painkillers and cuppa?'

'I'll get them thanks.' Clover said as she pushed herself up into a standing position, her bruised stomach muscles felt like they were being ripped apart with every movement. 'I could do with moving a bit and going to the bathroom.'

'Well, you take it easy up those stairs. It's always worse in the morning when you're recovering.'

Clover's feet dragged, her body weak and shaking with each step she took up the stairs. The banister became her support as her trembling hands clutched at it. With great effort, she managed to make it to the top of the staircase and into the bathroom. Leaning heavily on the side of the sink, she slowly lowered herself down onto the closed toilet seat. A faint smile crept across her lips as she realized how grateful she was for the tiny space of this bathroom in contrast to her own flat; she had no idea how she would manage there. She grabbed her toothbrush and began brushing her teeth, leaning over the sink. The thought of her flat brought back reminders that kept nagging at her - she really needed to get in touch with Rob one way or another today. By the time she'd finished having a wash, changed her clothes and made her way back down the stairs, she had made a decision - speaking to him was now her only task for the day.

'I've made you a cuppa downstairs.' Emma's voice interrupted her thoughts, as she called through the bathroom door. 'I'm heading off to bed now, that night shift was a killer.'

'Thanks mum.' Clover replied.

Hearing her mum's bedroom door shut, Clover made her way downstairs to drink her tea. Finally feeling like a bit better in herself she decided to head over to see if Ed has any news about her car.

Twenty-Seven

Clover stepped out of her house. She trudged towards Ed's shop, despite feeling better in the house, exhaustion quickly began weighing on every step, until finally she reached the entrance and pushed open the door.

A bell chimed from above as she entered, and Ed glanced up from his phone screen.

"Hey you!" He said, a smile played at his lips. "I've just this minute had a message from my mate, I was telling you about." Clover's spirits lifted at the news.

'Has he found anything out?' She asked, hope fluttering in her chest.

'He's found the address of the compound,' Ed replied. 'Said no belongings are ever removed from the vehicles and to call this number to arrange a time to go and collect what you need to do.' He handed her a scrap of paper with a number written in his unmistakable scrawl.

'That's brilliant. Thanks Ed. Do you mind if I use your phone?'

'Of course not.' Ed replied while looking suspiciously over her shoulder. 'I tell you what, why don't you go into the back and use it?'

Clover took the phone and rushed into the backroom, barely managing to close the door before he heard the bell of the shop tinkle as someone entered. Opening the paper Ed gave her, she presses the power button on the phone to begin dialling, before releasing that the phone was still locked. After trying a few combinations without luck, Clover was about to open the door when she heard raised voices coming from outside.

'You're telling me, you've never heard of her?' a stern voice asked from beyond the door.

'Nope. Never.' Ed replied, his words flat and curt. 'Now, if you don't mind, I need to get on with work.'

'I tell you what. If your memory ever does come across the name, then you give me a call yeah?' The man's tone had changed from frustrated to smug. Upon hearing the shop bell indicate that the door had been opened, heard it shut she then went out to Ed.

'Everything ok?' He asked, placing something into his back pocket.

'Who was that?'

'Just a customer. Did you manage to call the compound?'

'Er, the phones locked. Can you unlock it for me?'

As Ed punched in his passcode, Clover looks out on the street to see the stranger climbing into his car. Clover felt a familiar prickling at the base of her neck. She had seen this man somewhere before; she was sure of it. Martha had always said to trust your intuition and never ignore it – and now Clover's gut was telling her that something was very wrong with the situation. Taking the phone from Ed, she nervously stepped back into the office, tapping her foot as she waited for someone to answer her call. Her possessions were out there, somewhere – and unless she got them back soon, things would only get worse.

'Hertfordshire police compound.' The voice on the end of the call announced. No hello. No how can I help you.

Clover found herself stuttering, trying to explain her situation, and wanting to know how to receive her items.

'I'll be honest, Mrs Taylor, the car is in no fit state to be driving away. Ideally you will need to seek a recovery truck to come and collect it. There is a release charge of £250, but you can come and collect your belongings whenever you like. There's no release charge for them.'

'That's fine, I don't know what to do with the car yet, until I've spoken to the insurance, but I could really do with coming to collect my things.'

'No problem at all. I do have to warn you, we allow a 10-day free charge period, and then after that there is a daily charge rate. I will also need your permission to go and collect your belongings from the vehicle, as we can't authorise you to enter the yard and the vehicle yourself.'

'Okay, yes that's fine. When can I collect?'

'Any time after 1pm today. I will get everything bagged up and ready for collection.'

Passing on her thanks, Clover writes down the address and ends the call. She's sure she can hear talking again out the front, so opens the door slightly to listen.

'Like I told the man before, I don't know her.' Ed's voice was soft but strained as he spoke quietly to the person in the shop.

She leaned forward, trying to make out the rest of their conversation. But it wasn't long before she heard the bell and the door close again. She quickly pushed the address into her jean pocket and hurried back to the shop front. Luckily, Ed was preoccupied with another customer. She placed his phone on the counter, hastily pulled her hood up over her head, and left without saying a word. Instinctively, she knew they must be journalists - but why they were there remained a mystery. Adrenaline coursed through her veins as she rushed down the road, avoiding eye contact with anyone else. Before too long she had grabbed the keys to her mother's car and was speeding away from town. Her stomach churned at the prospect of driving, and it wasn't until after she had passed Glen Peaks' Village sign that she felt compelled to pull over. She slowly exhaled and took several deep breaths, allowing them to centre her focus on her breathing and then on her surroundings. It suddenly occurred to her that the number of cars going in and out of Glen Peaks seemed to have increased overnight - signalling something strange going on in town. With newfound determination, Clover shifted into first gear and pulled onto the main road towards the compound.

Twenty-Eight

The man behind the counter with a name badge of 'Tom' handed her a small blue crate. The type of crate you'd receive if you were to order an online grocery delivery.

'That's all we could find in the vehicle.' He said, shoving a clipboard at her with a piece of paper on it. 'Just sign here please, to say you've received everything.'

Clover took a quick look in the box, her laptop bag was there, her handbag and her small suitcase. Nothing looked open, so she signed the paperwork, hoping that everything was still in the bags.

'Do you need any help carrying it out?'

'I'm fine thanks.' Clover replied, lifting the box up, the muscles in her stomach burned as she did. Thankfully she had parked right outside the entrance, as her body struggled to hold the weight of everything.

'Leave it by the front door when you're done,' the man barked from the desk before the door slammed shut behind her. Undeterred, Clover opened the boot of her mother's hatchback and heaved the heavy plastic crate inside. As soon as her task was complete, she rifled through her bag for her phone—only to find that it wasn't there. Dropping everything else onto the pavement, she started throwing all of her belongings out of the crate in search of it. Finally, buried at the bottom, there it was in a clear plastic bag—undamaged but with a flat battery. With no in-car charger, Clover slammed shut the boot and dragged herself into the driver's seat in frustration. Putting her mother's car back into first gear, she set off on the long drive home.

Clover took a deep breath of relief as she pulled up to her mum's house; the traffic had been mercifully light on her drive back. There seemed to be less people visiting Glen Peaks than when she left, but she still yanked her hood up over her head as she stepped out of the car and hefted her bags from the boot.

No sooner had the door shut than Clover heard an anxious voice call out from the kitchen. 'Where have you been? I've been worried sick! Ed didn't know, nobody could contact you, and my car was missing too!'

'I went to get my stuff out the car.' Clover said defensively, holding up her phone as if to prove a point.

'You mean to say, you drove in my car, while on strong painkillers, just to get your phone?'

Clover wasn't in the mood to be treated like a juvenile teenager, so instead opted to ignore her, as she rummaged through her other bags looking for the charger.

'I can't believe it, Clover. You could have had another accident.'

'Well, I didn't.' Clover stropped off, finally finding her charger, and storming off to the kitchen to plug it in. She stood waiting patiently for the apple logo to appear on the screen. Piercing the painkiller packet and filling up a glass of water while she waited.

'Something's wrong.' She finally admitted, resting her head in her hands. She was also positive the phone never normally took that long to start up. 'There were journalists in Ed's shop this morning. I'm sure there were.'

'Oh, don't be silly.' Emma reassured. 'Ed popped over not long ago and not once did he mention about journalists.'

'Don't you dare tell me it's silly!' Clover spat out, her voice trembling with rage. 'And where is Rob? It's like he doesn't care that his wife's grandmother died and then she has an accident! He hardly calls me anymore, when I need him the most!'

Emma was taken aback by the ferocity of Clover's outburst. Her eyes blazed with indignation.

'I'm sure he has a good explanation for all this,' Emma tried to console her, 'you know how busy he is at work right now.' The notifications on Clover's phone lit up her face, momentarily breaking up the conversation. She scrolled through them quickly, her finger moved with a kind of forced precision to dismiss multiple emails and random social media notifications. There were a few messages from friends asking if she was okay, as they had heard about the accident. Then there were the ones from her agent demanding she call him. But nothing from Rob. With an uncomfortable tightening in her chest, she found his number and hit call without any hesitation. The second it went to voicemail, her finger stabbed at the screen repeatedly until finally 12 calls had been made. In a last effort of desperation, she tried his work number.

'Hello, Claudia speaking.' The voice on the end of the phone announced. 'How may I help you?'

'Hi Claudia, it's Clover. Can I speak to Rob please?'

The phone line went silent for a couple of seconds, and she could hear paper shuffling around in the background.

'Erm Rob?' Claudia repeated. 'Sorry he's not here at the moment.'

'Where is he?'

'You know I can't tell you that Clover.'

'Yes, you can, I'm his wife. You know that.'

'Sorry Clover, I need to go.'

Before Clover could react, the phone line went dead. She felt a jolt of fear run through her veins, and as she reached for the receiver to redial, her hand stopped in mid-air. Taking a deep breath, Clover decided to try calling her agent instead.

'Yes?' he bellowed into the phone.

'It's Clover.' She declared with a strong voice.

'Well, Well, Well. The wanderer replies.' His rage seemed to reverberate down the line as his words pierced through her. 'Where the bleeding hell have you been? I have been trying to phone you every day since God knows when.'

'Where's Rob?' Clover growled, refusing to answer his inquiries.

'I don't know where he is Clover. But I take it you haven't seen the news while you've been AWOL?'

'No, of course I haven't, you know I don't read or look at the news.'

She could hear him sighing down the phone line, rubbing his temples with stress. He then breathed out a puff of air.

'I think you should start there. I don't know, maybe at the beginning of last week.'

'What's going on?' Clover demanded again, her heart beating faster, as the sense of dread comes over her.

'Read the news. Then you'll understand. But listen Clover, there's not much I can do for you here now. I'll send your final cheque in the post for anything owing to you.'

Clover's throat tightened and her pulse quickened as she listened to the news on the other end of the line. 'What do you mean?' She begged, desperation rising in her voice.

But all she got in response was a cold, curt reply: 'I'm sorry to do this Clover, but I'm terminating your contract.'

Before Clover could even try to comprehend what had happened, He hung up abruptly, leaving her standing still in shock.

She turned slowly around to face Emma, tears streamed down her cheeks. Her voice quivering with fear and disbelief as she began to speak. 'What's happening?'

'What did he say?' Emma asked, placing a caring arm around her shoulders and pulling her into a hug.

'He's terminated my contract. He doesn't know where Rob is, and he's told me to check the news if I want to find out what's going on.'

'Oh Clover, I'm so sorry sweetie. Do you want to check the news? I'm sure it can't be that bad.'

'I'm scared mum.' Clover admitted, 'I don't know what's happening anymore.'

'I tell you what,' Emma said, rising from the kitchen table and placing a hand on Clover's shoulder. 'You go into the living room. I'll make us a pot of tea and we'll find out together, eh?' Clover nodded; her stomach tight with anticipation. She could already hear the sound of the kettle beginning to boil as she crossed the threshold into the living room. Grabbing her laptop from the bags she'd dumped by the front door when she came in, she settled herself comfortably on the sofa.

'Are we not putting the tv on?' Her mum asked, as she entered with a tray laden with a teapot, cups and a plate of biscuits.

'We need to use google. My agent said, it would be best to start off from the beginning of last week.'

Clover bit her lip as she fired up her laptop. She stared at the screen for a few moments, almost afraid to type in the words that would give her answers. Finally mustering the courage, she typed her name into Google's search bar and hit enter. Instantly a long list of websites and articles populated the page. The first one read: *'Has the lucky Clover finally lost her luck?'* Another screamed *'Clover in major road traffic accident on motorway.'* Her heart sank as she scrolled further down the list and came across an article titled *'Has Clover been seen in the village of Glen Peaks?'* She knew immediately who was behind this story—the journalists she had encountered earlier that day.

"What is there?" Emma asked impatiently.

Clover continued scanning the page until a headline caught her eye. Curiosity got the better of her, and without further hesitation she clicked on it.

Has Robert Taylor really ditched his lucky Clover for the younger model?

Clover felt a sudden chill run through her body, and she couldn't move as she read the words 'affair' and 'secret dates' on the laptop screen. She knew if she kept reading, her panic would only increase, so she quickly closed the laptop and placed it away. Her hands were shaking visibly, and she curled up in the chair, desperately trying to calm herself down before facing her mother's questioning gaze. Taking deep breaths, she slowly lifted her cup of tea to her lips, savouring its warmth as she slowly gathered her thoughts.

'Well, I now know where Rob has been all this time, and the reason he's been avoiding me.'

'What do you mean?' Emma replied, still confused as to what was going on. 'Where has he been?'

'It seems, he has been busy fucking the person who I thought was one of my good friends.'

Emma gasped, Clover wasn't sure if it was the swearing or the revelation which made her do it.

'Who?'

'Rachel. You only met her a couple of times.'

'Not the young dumb blonde from your party?'

Emma couldn't help but laugh. 'The very one! I can't believe I didn't see it before.'

Clover could feel the anger start flowing through her body, and she now found herself pacing the living room.

'After all this time, I really believed he was working.' Her voice cracked at the same time as rising in volume. 'All the times I made excuses for him, all the times I thought it was fine he wasn't here for me. Because I thought he was working!'

Clover watched her mother as she fiddled with the hem of her sweater and tried to formulate a response. Gathering up the half-finished cups of tea, Clover took them into the kitchen, blinking back

tears as she busied herself with washing them. With a heavy heart, she called out from the kitchen, 'I'm going out.'
'Are you sure that's wise?' her mum's voice called through from the living room.
'I'm fine!' Clover called, 'I'll go gentle.'
She pulled on her trainers, and opened the back door.

Twenty-Nine

Clover jumped at the sound of a voice from behind her, and spun around to see Ed. She opened her mouth to ask how he'd found her when he said softly, 'Your mum figured you'd be here.'

She felt her shoulders relax; there was something soothing about this little corner of Hope Cottage that she had loved since childhood. It was tucked away at the back of the garden, only accessible via a narrow footpath, away from prying eyes.

Ed smiled as his gaze swept over the lush grasses and wildflowers beneath them. 'Did you know' She began, 'This is where my mother found a four-leaf clover the day before I was born? That's where the name came from.'

'No, I didn't.' Ed replied, gently taking a seat next to her, pulling off his rucksack, which he carried to work. Watching the brook babble over the rocks in front of them, he stayed silent.

'I've always wanted to find another one, you know, to kind of prove that I'm not as unique and special as everyone makes out.'

'And have you?'

'No, I haven't. I used to sit for what seemed like hours as a child. On my hands and knees, just searching and searching.'

Ed rummaged through his backpack and pulled out a white bakery box, handing it to her with a smile. 'I got you this. Your mum figured you hadn't eaten yet.'

Clover smiled in appreciation before opening the box. A chuckle escaped her lips when she saw what was inside—a four-leaf clover biscuit made of butter and topped with green icing. She looked up at Ed, whose face was lit up with confidence. 'You were talking about catering to the tourists the other day, weren't you? This is your genius creation?' Ed nodded, still beaming from ear to ear.

Taking a bite of the cookie, Clover savoured the sweet taste.

'Well, looks like I've found my clover.' She replied, smiling back at him, taking a bite into it. 'And it's delicious!'

Ed then pulled out a flask and two disposable cups from the shop.

'I also thought you could do with a cuppa.'

'Great.' Clover replied. 'Although, I feel I could do with something a bit stronger.'

'Tea first, eat first, then maybe we can sort the stronger out later. Once you're off the painkillers.'

Clover watched as he filled two cardboard cups with hot tea from a thermos. He pulled small packets of milk and sugar from his bag, stirring them into the drinks. Handing the cup to Clover, she could see it in his eyes that he knew what she was about to ask. She reassured him, 'It's okay—everyone else knew before me too.'

He averted her gaze and busied himself by packing everything away back into his bag. 'I stopped reading the papers when you arrived,' he confessed. 'From our first conversation, I just knew you didn't have a clue what happened. I didn't want to be the one to tell you...but then there was the accident, and I knew you still wanted him to come back to you. I knew he wouldn't, but I just couldn't bring myself to break your heart like that.'

'It's fine, really Ed.' Clover placed a hand on his arm for reassurance. 'It wasn't your place to tell me, and I respect that.'

'What are you going to do now?'

'Ideally, sit out here and ignore everything.'

'But really?'

'I'm not sure. I really aren't. Rob hasn't answered any of my calls for ages, His P.A won't put me through to him. Now I don't even want to talk to him. I don't even know what to do. All of my stuff is back at the flat, which I don't want to go back to. So yes, I think I'll stay right here, just for a little bit longer.'

'Do you mind if I stay?'

Clover smiled at him. 'I'd love it if you'd stay. But only if you help me find another clover, I feel I need one more than ever right now to restore my luck.'

'I'll do my best!'

They both turned over, laying onto their stomachs, and started combing through the grass. Ed wasn't sure if clovers could be found in this particular patch, but he searched anyway. After giving up on finding a four-leaf luck charm, they both lay back and watched the clouds drift slowly across the sky. A contented sigh escaped from Ed's lips as he took in his surroundings.

'It really is peaceful here.'

Clover nodded in agreement before continuing. 'I can see why everyone falls in love with it. As a kid I was never bored, there were always new places to explore, but as a teenager I guess I didn't appreciate it as much. Once I left for college, I rarely thought about this place until now. Now I know I'd miss it.'

'You could stay, you know.'

'Stay where? With my mum forever.'

'Here, live in Hope Cottage.'

Clover let out a long breath and closed her eyes. Since her grandma's death, followed by the car accident, she hadn't even considered who had inherited this little house. She'd always assumed it would be left to her mother, surely her mother wouldn't want to live here on her own. She had always expressed such love for her own little house.

'I don't even know what I'm going to do for work. Let alone afford a house. My agent has been hinting for a while yet that I'm getting too old for my job. And now he's ditched me completely. Finding a new agent isn't going to be easy.'

'Things will sort itself out, they always do. But you should really consider living here.'

'We should really consider getting that stronger drink.' Clover smiled. 'Do you think it's safe to go back?'

'What do you mean?'

'As in, did you see any journalists when you came up?'

'There was a few. Here wear this.' Pulling off his work hoody, Clover slipped it on over her head, taking in Ed's comforting sense. Pulling up the hood, she turned to look at him.

'How do I look?'

'Not suspicious at all.' He laughed. 'Come on, let's go dodge some Journalists. Then what do you says? Takeaway and a bottle of wine for me and a diet coke for you?'

Clover pouted as she remembered the lack of drinking due to the painkillers. 'A diet coke sounds perfect!'

As they made their way down the hill, Clover couldn't help but cast an appreciative eye over Hope Cottage. The garden was a tangle of weeds, with plants growing up against the greenhouse, and a rotten fence running along the edge of the property. But in her mind's eye, she could see it transformed into something special; her own little piece of peaceful bliss.

Heading down the road, back to her mother's cottage, Ed suddenly came to a stop as he noticed the small group of people gathered outside her house. His expression darkening at sight of them.

'How did they find out where I lived?' Clover asked shockingly.

'I don't know.' Ed replied seriously, 'But you can't go back there. Look, come back to mine, it's just round the corner and we'll give your mum a call.'

'Somebody must have told them where you lived.' Clover ranted to her mother over the phone, her glass of coke already in her hand. She really needed something stronger, but Ed was busy finding the takeaway menu.

'I don't know who would do something like that.' Her mother said, the ever naïve. 'But you stay with Ed tonight, I'm on a night shift anyway. Hopefully, they would have got bored and will be gone by tomorrow.'

'You obviously don't know journalists.' Clover sighed back through the phone. 'But hopefully you're right.'

Just as Clover hung up, Ed entered the room, hands empty of takeaway menus.

'I must have thrown them all out.' He confessed, 'But we'll just order online. What do you fancy?'

Thirty

Clover stirred, groggily lifting her head off the pillow. She had spent the night in Ed's guest room come small home office. The room was a cosy affair of an overstuffed armchair, bookshelves and a small guest bed. At some point during their night Clover had kicked off her shoes, leaving them strewn across the floor alongside empty wine bottles and discarded food wrappers. She had finally convinced Ed to let her have a glass of wine after pointed out that she hadn't had any painkillers since that morning. Reaching out to grab her phone, she noticed how quiet it was - typically at this time, she would be woken to a variety of notifications from her social media platforms. With a heavy heart, she unlocked the screen and saw only one message from her mother. Opening it up, it read:

Journalists not here, going to bed now. Mum xxx

Clover smiled to herself, not only was it great that the journalists had given up for now. But her mother's messages always made her smile. Straight to the point. Deciding not to message back, for not wanting to wake her, she pulled herself out of bed. Leaving her phone behind, she cautiously stepped into the hallway, careful to not disturb Ed's sleep. To her surprise, he was already in the kitchen, a pot of coffee brewed, and the smell of freshly baked croissants wafted through the air.

'Do you normally get up this early?' Clover smiled to him, as he handed her a ready poured coffee.

'Some of us, have work to do.' He grinned back, 'The ovens need turning on and everything baking.'

'Give me five minutes, and I'll leave with you.' She said, feeling guilty that he had so much to do.

'Seriously, it's fine. You take your time, have a nice breakfast. Just lock the door behind you.'

'Are you sure?' Clover quizzed. She didn't know if she felt comfortable enough to stay in his flat by herself. 'I really won't be long, Mum messaged to say that there's no journalists outside, so I'll head back there as soon as I'm ready.'

Ed hadn't wanted to tell her, that last night while she was on the phone to her mother, and he was supposedly looking for takeaway menus. He was in fact on the phone to his mate in the police force, asking if he could do something about the journalists. He was pleased that it seemed to have worked, for now anyway.

'That's great.' Ed replied, looking at his watch. 'Look, I've really got to go. But I'll see you later yeah?'

'Yeah, super. Thanks a lot Ed. Really, for everything.'

Ed offered a shy smiled and grabbed his work bag.

'It's no problem at all. See you later.'

Clover barely had time to reply, before he was out of the door, and it closed behind him. Feeling slightly awkward, Clover tried to think back on the previous night's conversation, hoping she didn't go on too much about Rob. Drinking her coffee, while she sat at the breakfast bar, she took in her surroundings. Compared to her flat back in the city, this was half the size, yet seemed so much more welcoming than hers. It was clean, neutral but still had personal touches of Ed's personality. Pictures of people who she assumed were friends and family, were hung in different sized frames, creating a picture wall along the main hallway. The living room area was simple, yet homely, with just a tv, sofa, chair and a table. Her flat that she shared with Rob, had so much in it, yet nothing that reflected her personality. Instead, it was filled with impressive pieces of art and deco ornaments, which she actually had no care for at all. There were also three double bedrooms, and a smaller office room. Which after looking at Ed's house, and living back at her mum's cottage, were all completely unnecessary to have for just two adults.

Draining her cup, she pulled open the dishwasher and added it to the pile of plates which needed washing. She covered up the spare croissants and headed back into the bedroom to change, collecting her phone and all her other belongings before leaving. Taking a detour on her way to her mum's house, Clover wanted to walk past Hope Cottage one more time just to see if the feelings she felt yesterday were still there.

The white picket fence fashioned the peeled paint affect as she pushed it open. The stone path from the gate to the front door was covered in moss and weeds and the single glazed windows with wooden frames looked like they were rotting. Glancing over past the side of the house, Clover saw the greenhouse she had envisioned herself growing vegetables in yesterday. Though it had broken panes of glass and looked like it needed a tidy up, she was sure she could make it work. Making her decision, Clover turned on her heal and headed back to her mother's place with a renewed sense of purpose.

Clover breathed out a sigh of relief when she turned the corner of the road and noticed no journalists were hanging around. It seemed that for today, Glen Peaks, was back to its normal quiet self. The normal quiet self, that Clover had begun to enjoy. Pushing open the cottage door, the house was still quiet as her mother slept off her night shift from the day before. Closing the door behind her quietly, she grabbed her laptop, turned it on and instantly began her planning.

By the time her mother appeared, hair ruffled and sleepy faced. Clover was still typing furiously away at the laptop. Pieces of paper were strewn all around her, with notes added to them in her scruffy writing.

'Tea?' her mother asked, baffled and unsure what was going on.

'Please.' Clover mumbled, 'Then I'll fill you in.'

'Right.' Emma replied, quickly exiting the room to do what she knew best.

As Emma brought in the tray of biscuits and tea, Clover was just piling her papers together and setting her laptop aside.

'What's all this then?' Emma asked cautiously.

'I've been thinking. Well to be honest, Ed brought it up first, and I wasn't too sure. But then it got me thinking and I think he's right.' Clover mumbled on, while Emma sat there patiently waiting. 'But I've been sat here all morning, going over everything and I think it's doable, I really do.'

Emma sensed the excitement within Clover's voice and was pleased. She was worried yesterday when she left for work, and she hadn't seen her all day. She certainly didn't expect this turn of events.

'I want to buy Hope Cottage.' Clover finally blurted out. 'I've looked, and I reckon with my half of the flat from Rob, I easily will have enough to buy it and do it up.'

'Hope Cottage? You want to buy it?' Emma was baffled, she always has the sense the Clover couldn't wait to get away from the place, let alone wanting to move there.

'I do.' Clover beamed, 'I want to stay here, and I want to do Hope Cottage up and live there and grow my own vegetables.'

Emma laughed, really laughed. 'You don't know how to grow vegetables.' She said in between pauses.

Clover began laughing too, till tears were streaming down her face and her stomach muscles ached. She wasn't sure if they were tears she'd been holding back, or tears of pure joy. 'I'm going to learn.'

'This is great, Clover, it really is. I'd love nothing more than having you back here all the time. But you need to be sure?'

'I'm sure. I've never felt so sure of anything in my life. Here is where I want to be. Hope Cottage is where I'm at my best. I can start a fresh, be myself and live the life I want.'

Emma stood up and left the room, after hearing some rummaging in the kitchen, she came back in. Handing a set of keys to Clover, she had tears in her own eyes.

'Hope Cottage is yours.' She announced, 'June left the cottage to you. The solicitor rang yesterday but I wanted to tell you face to face.'

Clover found herself shaking with shock.

'Are you serious?'

'I am Clover, I was going to tell you today anyway. But I didn't expect all of this.' She said waving her arms at the mess Clover at made with her lists of paper.

'Well, if that isn't the world telling me I'd made the right decision, then I don't know what is.' Clover breathed out a sigh of relief. 'And this means, all the money from the flat, can go straight into the renovations.'

Thirty-One

The bell above the door jingled as she stepped into Ed's shop, which always brought back a flood of memories from her childhood. 'Hello?' she called out to the empty shop.

'In here,' was the muffled response from behind a door leading off the shop. She followed the scent of freshly baked goods until she reached the kitchen. Gleaming steel ovens lined one wall, while fridges and shelves filled with baskets and boxes filled another. In the middle stood a small island was where Ed kneaded dough, wearing a stained apron and covered in flour.

'Well, this looks interesting.' Clover exclaimed. 'I can't believe I never knew you actually did all of this.'

Ed laughed. 'How did you think all the bread and cakes got here?'

'I thought you brought them in.'

'Really?' Ed continued, as he shaped the dough into a ball, placed it into a bowl and covered it up. 'You seriously thought I'd just own a bakery and buy the goods in?'

Wiping down the surfaces, he focused on Clover.

'You seem cheerful today.'

'I am actually.' Clover replied, a grin plastered across her face.

'Care to share?'

'I've got a few things to do, and I'll fill you in. Do you fancy going out for a drink later?'

'Why not?' Ed grinned back.

Clover grinned and nodded. 'Brilliant, I'll meet you over the pub about seven-ish.' The door shut behind her, and Clover made her way up to Hope Cottage with the keys firmly tucked into her pocket. She took a deep breath before unlocking the door and pushing open the door. She was immediately hit by the musty smell that often accompanied unlived-in houses. Despite her mother checking on the house every couple of days, it still managed to accumulate that stale odour. Clover made a mental note to buy some scented candles once she was settled in.

Looking around, she knew there was a lot of work to be done. Her plan was to go back to her flat for her personal belongings but leave all the furniture. It never suited her taste, but at least Hope Cottage was fully furnished for now.

As she inspected each room, she pulled out her notebook and wrote down what needed to be repaired or replaced. Some things were more than thirty years old, like the old units that June had whitewashed a good fifteen years ago – they had now turned an unpleasant yellow colour, but they were sturdy and solid.

Butterflies danced in Clover's stomach as she imagined sanding down the cabinets and giving them new life with a fresh coat of paint. It would take time and effort, but she could already envision how it would transform the space. Every step she took throughout the room, made her see the potential and made her realise how much she was looking forward to living the next part of her chapter.

She frowned at the thought of having to contact Rob, knowing it was something she didn't want to do. But if she wanted this cottage to become home, then she had no choice.

The sun began to set as Clover locked up Hope Cottage and headed towards the pub where her Ed waited for her.

Sitting in the pub later that evening, Clover looked at the notification tone on her phone alerted her to a message.

Be there in a min, Ed x

She smiled to herself, it had only just gone 7pm, so he really wasn't late at all. Yet he felt the need to message her and let her know. Placing her cardigan over her chair, so people knew the table was taken. Clover made her way to the bar, where she ordered both her and Ed a drink.

Ed arrived, looking like he'd ran most of the village.

'Brill, you got drinks.' He puffed, taking a big gulp.

'Are you ok?' Clover laughed, normally he was always so calm and collected, she wasn't used to seeing this side of him.

'Try having a flour delivery and rushing around unloading it at 6.30pm.' He explained, taking another sip of his drink.

'Tell me more.' Clover asked, 'I never knew this side of you before. I know what brought you to Glen Peaks, but not before then.'

'My mum, used to work in a local bakery. I used to have to be there early in the mornings before school. You know being the single mum life, I had no other choice. Secretly I hated it. Having to get up before 6am every morning to head down to her work, where I'd sit. The only bonus was, we always ended up with free breakfast, and leftover cakes and breads which didn't sell. As I grew older, I began working there, to earn my own pocket money. The owner used to say, that if I was coming to work with her, then I might as well make myself useful. I started off by doing the jobs nobody wanted to do; the cleaning, the pot washing, and then I moved onto making the mixture up. At first, I thought I'd hate it, but then I developed a strange sense of love, of watching these mixes turn into creations which everyone loved.'

Clover watched in admiration, as he talked so passionately about his early life.

'When I left school, and it came to me getting a real job. I ended up working in some bars, you know how young lads straight out of school often did. But that wasn't where I wanted to be, there was no enjoyment pulling pint after pint, and clearing up after the drunk. I wormed my way into the kitchens and ended up gaining an apprenticeship to become a chef. However, once I qualified, I realised that the chef lifestyle wasn't for me. The hours are ridiculous, the turnaround times and workload are too. When I visited Glen Peaks for the first time, something suddenly dawned on me what I wanted and what I needed to do. I got home and started researching properties, and as they say, the rest his history.'

'I find it fascinating.' Clover admitted, 'Hands down, I never ever would have had you down for a baker.'

'What would you have me down for?' Ed laughed back.

'Oh, I don't know, some marketing expert, some kind of office job.'

'Definitely not. I could never spend my day sat at a desk. Besides, enough about me. What's your news?'

For the next half an hour, Clover's words escaped her lips in a flurry of excitement as she described all her future plans with gusto; a passion that Ed displayed every time he spoke about his own career. It was then that it hit her, something she hadn't realised had been missing; she was alive and energised by her ideas. Finishing the last sip of her drink, Clover smiled widely.

'So that's that!'

'That's great,' Ed gushed, his smile filling up the room. 'It would be so wonderful to have you back in the village full time.' He paused and glanced away briefly before turning back, taking a more serious tone. 'But I hate to ask this, but what about Rob?'

'I'm going to be honest here, cards on the table and all that malarkey. When I found out about the affair, it wasn't anger or upset I was feeling because of what he did, but almost for me being so stupid that I hadn't noticed. Easily for the last 6 months, even a year, we've hardly spent any time together. The fact that he couldn't be here for when June died meant that he didn't care. The funny thing is, I wasn't too bothered that he wasn't here either. Looking back, we'd drifted apart far too long ago, so how can I be sad or upset over something that wasn't even there? If anything, he's released me from a life I didn't know I needed releasing from.'

'That's great, it really is. I'll be honest, I was worried when your mum called me. But you're stronger than I thought.'

Clover smiled at him, their eyes making the perfect eye contact.

'Another drink to celebrate?' Ed broke the silence.

'Why not?'

As Ed headed over to the bar, Clover pulled out her phone and opened up her emails. Her heart raced as she waited for a reply from Rob, with whom she had tried to call earlier but he had refused to speak to her. Instead, she opted for sending him an email - one that clearly stated she accepted a mutual separation and asked for him to coordinate the sale of their flat, with half of the value going to her. She tapped her foot nervously against the wooden floor of the now empty pub while willing her phone to buzz in response, yet it remained silent.

Ed eventually returned with two glasses clinking lightly between his hands. He placed them down onto the table.

'Another question, what's your plans for the future? Do you intend on modelling still?'

'I haven't thought that far. I'm very lucky that I do have a nice little nest egg in the bank already, and hopefully with the sale of the flat, after the renovations, I'll have enough to last a little longer.'

'Cheers to that.' Ed said, holding his glass up so she could share the cheers and chink his. 'I'm really pleased. Really pleased.'

They continued the rest of the night talking about future plans for Hope Cottage, Clover, and Ed himself. They were only interrupted when the bell rang behind the bar signalling last orders.

'This is beginning a bit of a habit.' Ed laughed, as him and Clover exited the pub together.

Thirty-Two

Clover stood in the sunlit living room, taking in the empty space. The walls were stripped to their original plaster, and she had hauled away old pieces of furniture and tattered curtains to make way for her renovations. At the funeral a week ago all the locals asked what was happening with Hope Cottage and were delighted when Clover filled them in on her plans. Now everyone seemed to be settling back into life as normal, or at least as close to normal as it could be with June gone.

She heard the front door open, and Ed stepped in carrying two steaming mugs of coffee and two muffins. He had been coming over every day after work for the past week, bringing whatever leftovers hadn't sold that day from his bakery. His footsteps echoed loudly in the hollow house, and Clover smiled at him gratefully before heading out to greet him.

'It looks massive.' He observed entering the living room, which was the last room to be emptied. 'I can't believe you did it all yourself.'

'Mum helped this morning.' She explained, taking the coffee from him. 'Besides, there actually wasn't as much in this room as the rest. Getting the carpet up was the hardest part.'

Ed took off his jacket, and rolled up his sleeves, ready to get to work. 'Right, so what's next on the list?'

Clover pulled the list out of her back pocket and scrolled down it with her index finger.

'It looks like we're in for a night off.'

'A night off? Really?' he asked in disbelief.

'Yep, looks like it. The next thing that needs doing is the plastering. He's coming in to give me a quote tomorrow, and until he's done, we can't do nothing more inside. I think I'll start on the garden next, or maybe start on the furniture in the workshop.'

'I'm all up for a night off.' Ed yawned, then smiled back at Clover.

'Gosh, I'm so sorry. Really you head home. You've been here all week; you must be shattered'.

'That I am. But I'm also hungry first. Let's go grab something to eat and then I'll get an early night.'

'Go out to eat? I can't go dressed like this. I'd need to get a shower and some clean clothes.'

Ed took in Clover's appearance, something he'd got used to all week, and he couldn't deny, he found her very attractive. Her hair was piled on top of her head, into a messy bun. Dressed in ripped jeans, and a black t-shirt, which were both covered in dust and God-knows what else. She was quite different from the model version of herself which had arrived just weeks before.

'No need for getting ready. I said, grab some food, not go out to eat. Come on, lock up. My car's on the drive.'

'Okaaay then.' Clover replied, eyeing him curiously. She was too hungry and too tired to argue. Leading the way out of the house, she then followed Ed down to his car. Climbing into the passenger seat, Clover's body relaxed instantly into it, as Ed started the car.

'So where are we going?'

'You'll see.' Ed replied, with a sly smirk.

As they drove, the winding country roads seemed to stretch on forever. Clover had hummed along to several songs before a particularly nostalgic one came on, and she found herself singing really loudly, feeling a bit silly but happy, nonetheless. Beside her, Ed grinned with amusement and joined in during the parts of the song he knew, making up funny words for the ones he didn't know. His goofy little display made Clover laugh louder than ever. Before long, Ed slowed down and pulled into a roadside layby with views stretching far out into the countryside. But when Clover saw a greasy-looking burger van next to them, she scrunched up her nose in disdain.

'We're not eating here?' Clover scoffed.

'Sometimes Clover, all you need in life is a good greasy burger, with plenty of onions and a good view to eat it in.'

'Alrighty then. But if I get food poisoning, I'm blaming you.'

Ed stepped up to the van, aware of Clover walking behind him. He took a few extra seconds to watch her as she meandered towards some of the picnic benches placed at the edge of the grass. She almost seemed to be smiling and it made Ed's heart swell with pride. The sight of her seemed to melt all the stress away, making her look younger and more relaxed.

"Two burgers please, both with onions," Ed told the server behind the counter. She nodded and moved quickly to prepare his order. Soon enough, Ed had two greasy burgers wrapped in napkins, their aroma wafting in the air.

'I'll grab two cokes too please.'

The server didn't even speak, as she turned, reached for the cans and placed them on the counter. Ed offered her a ten-pound note, and she worked quietly returning his change. Not even a smile, as Ed thanked her and headed over to Clover.

'Wow, a burger and a coke.' Clover smiled, as Ed reached her. 'Aren't I the lucky lady?'

'What can I say? I know how to treat them right.' He winked back, making butterflies in Clover's stomach come to life. She suppressed them quickly, focusing on the greasy mess which Ed handed to her. 'Trust me, you're going to love it.'

'I never had you down for the greasy van type of person. You know, all Mr seeded bread and healthy organic bakery.'

'Everyone has their weakness.' He grinned back, 'Plus everything in moderation, right?'

'Oh my god. This takes me right back to my teenage years.' Clover grinned, as she finished swallowing her first bite. 'It reminds me of this café me and my friends used to go to on a Saturday afternoon. I'd forgotten how good these tasted.'

'You're telling me, you haven't had a burger since a teenager?'

Clover shook her head, as she took another bite into her burger.

'What not even a McDonald's?'

Another shake of the head, as she continued to chew.

'Burger king? KFC?'

'You have to understand the industry.' Clover began when she'd finished chewing. 'I went into modelling from the age of 18. It's a dangerous world, where my body is my job. I had people scrutinising it, and me. Nobody in that sector could ever be seen eating anything but healthy foods. Then when I got with Rob, he was more body and health obsessed than I was. Even takeaways with friends or meals out, resulted in grilled vegetables and boiled rice. I just learned not to want it.'

'Well cheers to your first burger in many years.' Ed smiled, holding up his coke can.

'Cheers.' Clover replied, bashing hers into is. 'A full fat coke was always a big no! In fact, I probably haven't eaten so much of the food I was never allowed until I came back here. Thanks to you.'

'My pleasure.' Ed grinned, feeling slightly pleased with himself. 'And may I say, you're still looking exactly the same as you did when you first arrived.'

Ed bit down into his burger, causing onions to ooze out of the other side.

'That's disgusting.' Clover laughed, before reaching over and grabbing a some of the stray onions. 'But they are the best.'

'Talking of Rob. Have you heard from him?'

'Nothing at all. I'm hoping he's sorting something out with his solicitor.' Clover explained. 'My plan is to try and get in touch with him at the end of this week again, and if nothing then I'll have to try and get a solicitor to get in touch. It won't be long before I'll start needing the money from the flat.'

'Well hopefully you won't be needing to do that.' Ed reassured. 'Fingers crossed he sorts it out without needing any of that.'

'Fingers crossed.' Clover smiled, screwing up the now empty napkin which originally held her burger. 'I hate to say it but that was...'

'Delicious, right?' Ed finished for her. Ed copied her, in screwing up his napkin and gathering all the rubbish together. 'We better head back, I could do with an early night for once.'

'Too right. I could certainly do with a long hot bath! I've never felt so dusty in all my life.'

'You seem to be experiencing a lot of new things this week.' Ed jested with her.

Clover batted him playfully with her arm, as they headed back to the car.

Thirty-Three

Clover and Emma had worked tirelessly for over a week, the sun shining down on them like a blessing from above. Clover had managed to clear an old path of weeds with Ed's jet wash, and the garden gate had been realigned to open and close with ease. While Emma gave the gate a fresh coat of paint in sage green, Clover hauled out the old lawn mower from the shed and started tackling the long grass.

Suddenly, their hard work was rewarded when the plasterer called to say that he had a cancelled job and could fit them in right away. Everything seemed to be going according to plan.

With her phone in hand, Clover stepped back as far as possible and took a photo of her work so far; she had done this throughout each step of her home and garden makeover project. Opening up the messaging app, she quickly found Ed's stream of messages and sent him the picture.

Another day gardening xx

She typed, attaching the new picture to the message. It didn't take long at all before he replied.

Another day baking can't wait to see you later. Another greasy burger? Xx

Clover smiled to herself. She found herself smiling more each day when she was in contact with Ed.

Maybe, can't wait till I have a kitchen and I can cook you a proper meal xx

Secretly, she had loved the last couple of times they'd taken a drive out to their new favourite spot. At the weekend, they had gone purely just for a very watered-down coffee and a bacon roll.

'You'll never get that greenhouse finished, if you don't stop staring at your phone.' Emma interrupted her thoughts, smiling at her, as she knew all too well who she was messaging.

'Alright, alright.' Clover replied, slipping her phone back into the back pocket of her jeans.

Ed had given her a hand over the weekend, replacing all the broken glass panes of the greenhouse. Now that the structure was completely watertight thanks to their efforts, Clover grabbed her wheelbarrow from the side of the house and made her way inside the greenhouse. She was pleased to find that the hinges and mechanisms still worked perfectly. Inside, the heat was already building, so she wound the handle at the side of the door which opened up four windows on either side, letting in some welcoming fresh air. Pulling on a pair of gardening gloves, Clover started collecting broken pots into the wheelbarrow, throwing them one by one while memories of past times spent with Emma in the garden came flooding back. Once full, she pushed it over to a rented skip where Emma was finishing work on replanting some flower beds which she had recently emptied and replaced with new soil.

'We'll stop for a cuppa.' Her mum called, as she watched Clover head back over to the greenhouse for the third time.

'I've got biscuits in my bag.' Clover called back. 'From Ed.'

Clover knew, behind her back, Emma was grinning like a Cheshire cat.

Clover wiped the sweat off her forehead and tucked a loose strand of hair behind her ear. With one last glance around the greenhouse to check she hadn't missed any weeds; she grabbed the overflowing wheelbarrow and began slowly navigating the path up to the skip. As she rounded the corner, she caught sight of the postman walking up their drive. She smiled to herself as she remembered Ed's suggestion to redirect her mail to Glen Hopes. Taking a deep breath, she had taken the plunge and changed her forwarding address to Hope Cottage—her own little slice of heaven that was beginning to feel like home.

'These are for you I think, love.' The postman announced, handing a giant pile of letters, held together with blue elastic bands.

'Thanks.'

'You living here now?'

'I am.' Clover replied. 'It used to be my Nan and Grandad's house. Well, my Great Nan and Grandad, but my Nan lived here too.'

'Say, you're not bloody Clover, are you?'

'I am,' Clover eye suspiciously, as she did anytime somebody knew who she was.

'I can't believe it.' The postman puffed out a breath of air. 'I'm Alan, we went to school together.'

'Alan Starling?' Clover gasped, 'No way!'

She could not even picture the bald headed, stocky man who stood in front of her, as the small and weedy, curly haired boy that used to sit next to her in class.

'The very one.' He puffed out proudly. 'I always remember you saying you lived here, but never seen you around.'

'I've not been back long. But it's great to be back.'

'Everyone always comes back eventually. But I best get on. Nice seeing you again, no doubt I'll see you about more now mind.'

'You sure will.' Clover replied, thanking him for the post, as he headed off down the road back towards the town. Pulling off the elastic band, Clover quickly flicked through the pile of post. The usual bank statements, store card offers, and a few items of fan mail didn't stand out as unusual. She was looking for some correspondence from Rob, but then reminded her how he wouldn't send anything to their joint address. Realising he wouldn't know the address of Hope Cottage or her mums house, she decided that as soon as she was done at the house, she would start looking for solicitors. Him ignoring her was becoming too infuriating.

'Everything all right love?' Her mum interrupted her, holding two cups of tea in her hands.

'Post from the flat.' Clover waved it at her and sighed. 'I've decided, this evening I'll start looking for a solicitor. If he's not going to try and get in touch with me or reply to my calls, then I need to start it my end.'

'I think that would be the best idea. Tell you what, you can get off now if you'd like to get start?'

'Not really.' Clover replied honestly, 'I enjoy working in the garden, and I'm so close to finishing. I'll do a bit of research this evening.'

Luckily for Clover, it didn't take as long as she'd initially thought to finish the garden. Just before the first cloud of that week threatened to rain, she'd pushed the door open to Ed's shop.

'Well, this is a nice surprise.' He grinned, looking up from his laptop after hearing the bell ring on the door.

Clover smiled back, as she walked towards the counter grabbing one of her favourite muffins as she went past.

'I'm all done for now.' She announced, leaning on the counter. 'Shall we have a coffee?'

Turning around, Ed instantly turned on the shop coffee machine, grabbing two disposable cups from under the unit. Clover watched him while he worked, he always looked so relaxed and calm, either when he was just making drinks or baking his variety of cakes and breads. It was nice to watch. As he finished, and turned back around, Clover quickly glanced down at her phone.

'I'm searching for a solicitor.' She sighed, as he placed her drink in front of her. 'Don't reckon you know one?'

'As a matter of fact,' Ed smiled, and pulled his notepad across the desk. 'I had a feeling you'd be needing one, so I did a bit of research myself.'

Opening the notebook, he tore out a page he had clearly written on.

'Here are a few I found within the local area, some are bigger law firms, some are independent ones. But they do all seem to have great recommendations online.'

Clover took the list and scrolled down it with her eyes. She recognised a few of the bigger names, but only their names from adverts on tv or the local radio.

'This is great. Seriously, thank you. This has saved me a bunch of time.'

Thirty-Four

Pulling into the carpark, Clover looked up at the at the small row of buildings. She quickly spotted the one she needed; the small signage next to the door saying, 'Harper & James Family Law.' Taking one last look at her phone, in hopes that Rob had been in touch, she sighed to herself. Pushing open the car door, she climbed out.

'I've got an appointment at 10.30am.' Clover announced, as she reached the small desk. A petite woman, no older than twenty-four years old, perfectly manicured nails smiled at her, before looking at the screen.

'Name?'

'Mrs Harding.' She replied. It was Ed's idea not to give her first name, or even use her real surname. He'd been correct of course; she hadn't wanted to risk anything being leaked to the press before she was certain that they were the solicitors she wanted to use.

'Take a seat please, Mr James will be with you shortly.' Clover surveyed the cramped reception area as she entered. Two threadbare chairs were tucked in front of a foggy window, and an ancient water cooler hummed nearby on a stained carpet. She noticed a small table off to the side with a limp newspaper and some dog-eared magazines. With a sigh, she chose one of the chairs and pulled out her phone.

Just waiting to go in now xxx

She messaged Ed, then looked up to see the receptionist focusing on her, who quickly looked back at her computer screen, a quick smile flashed across her face.

Luckily, she wasn't waiting much longer before a young man came into the reception area.

'Mrs Harding?' He announced, looking directly at her. Being the only other person besides his employee in the room, Clover stood up directly and headed towards him. Holding out his hand for her to shake, he welcomed her. 'This way please.'

Entering into his office, Clover took a seat without being asked. While Mr James took the one opposite her, behind his desk.

'Now, tell me what can I do for you?' He asked, 'I remember you mentioning starting divorce proceedings. Yes?'

Clover spent the next couple of minutes explaining the situation she'd found herself in, without naming either her name or Robs.

'I see.' The solicitor replied, his hands steepled, fingertips connecting and elbows resting on the desk. 'Well, it seems pretty straight forward. We can file for divorce on the grounds of adultery from his side. If he agrees then it will all go through painlessly and then we will sort the remains of the property and the financial side.'

'Great, so what happens now?'

'If you're happy to go ahead. Then all we need are some contact details for him. We'll draft up a divorce agreement and settlement plan. This will then be sent to him, and he will have 14 days to reply. Depending on his reply, will depend on where we go from that. If what you say is true, then I don't know why he would dispute it.'

'Great. I also brought a copy of our marriage certificate as asked.'

'Brilliant, I take it you would like to go ahead then?'

'Yes please.' Clover replied nervously.

'Super. Let me just bring up the system and we'll take your details first, if you don't mind.'

Clover smiled weakly; this was the part she was dreading. Secretly she was hoping her solicitor lived under a rock and wasn't up to date with current affairs.

'Right, here we go. Your name please.'

'Mrs Clover Taylor.' She replied confidently. Watching him double take, and then looked down at his diary where his appointments were found.

'Not Mrs Harding?' He questioned.

'No sorry. Mrs Clover Taylor.'

She was impressed as he continued and asked no further questions. Instead taking all the details he needed, and not even flinching when she gave Mr Robert Taylor's name, who coincidentally lived in the main city.

'Well, it's nice to meet you.' Mr James said, as he guided her out of the office and into the main reception. 'I'll get everything we need filled in and send him notice that you would like to proceed with a divorce. Like I said before, he has 14 days to reply, so I'll be in touch when I hear anything. If I do.'

'That's great, it really is.' Clover replied, noticing her breathing feeling a lot lighter than it had done before.

'Well thanks for choosing Harper & James. Speak to you soon Mrs Harding.'

And just like that, he was heading back into his office. His choice of calling her by her alliance, took her by surprise. He never once acknowledged he knew who she was, yet using Mrs Harding to bid her farewell, seemed to indicate he knew full well the reason for using a fake name.

Thirty-Five

Clover and Ed sat in the garden surrounded by the remnants of their picnic. The sun was unusually warm for the time of year, and it cast an idyllic orange glow over the entire garden. The house loomed in the background; its interior walls now only partially covered by white plaster. Through the opened windows Clover could see where the plasterer had been working over the last week – heaps of bright white powder were scattered across the ground like snowdrifts, and a faint layer of dust coated every surface. Somewhere in the distance, they could hear the sound of a radio playing and a man singing out of tune but full-hearted. 'It certainly brings some life into the house,' Clover said with a laugh. 'I imagine it's quite strange being in such a big empty house on your own.'

'That's certainly true,' Ed replied.

'Growing up, the house always seemed busy. Almost like, every time I stepped into the kitchen there was someone new from the village sat at the table asking grandma for advice.' Clover smiled to herself at the memory. 'She was like the village oracle.'

'It sounds splendid.' Ed smiled back at her. 'Have you had any more thoughts for your future plans?'

'Oh, I've got a few. But first I just want to concentrate on getting the house complete. I don't think I could do anything, while this mess is still around me.'

'It'll be done before you know it.' Ed replied, always the positive. 'Although, I better think of getting back to the shop. I expect Jean will be waiting outside for her weekly top up of snacks.'

Clover stood with him, gathering the empty cups and plates. The sink still wasn't in use in the kitchen, so she was taking them back to her mums house every day to wash them.

'I'll walk back with you.' She announced, 'There's nothing more for me to do here, I'll just go let Mark know.'

Leaving the house, and heading down the garden gate, after telling Mark she was on her way home. Clover couldn't help but smile seeing Ed waiting for her. Despite him spending every lunch break with her, and most weekends, there was something about him which made her stomach flutter like a teenager whenever she saw him. She didn't know if he had the same feelings, however he equally too always seemed pleased to see her. He'd even joined her on one of her morning runs the other day.

'Ready?' He smiled back at her, as she approached.

'Ready.'

Leaving the gate and heading back down into the village, the way she had once done when she was a little girl, always brought a sense of happiness. Right now, in this moment, she had never felt more content with her life.

'What you up to for the rest of the day?' Ed interrupted her thoughts.

'I don't know, I need to pop out and do some shopping for the house, but it seems pointless when I've got nowhere for it to actually go yet. So, I might just take a long bath and put a good old romance movie on.'

'Sounds great. Well apart from the romance film.'

Clover batted him on his playfully. Secretly she wanted to invite him over, to watch some lame horror film he was obsessed with. However, she also knew the importance of not being too overbearing. Reaching the cottage, he passed her the bag of dirty plates and cup.

'You go enjoy your bath and film then. Others have work to do.' He said, sticking his bottom lip out like a sulking toddler.

'And what a shame that is. I'll have a great afternoon.' Clover replied, taking her key out of her bag, and sliding it into the lock. She wanted nothing more than to tell him how she wished he could join her but decided not to. Even on a playful level.

A silence fell between them both. Almost as if neither of them wanted to say goodbye, yet both knew their friendship wasn't at the level of where they expressed how they felt.

'I'll be seeing you then.' Ed broke the silence first. 'I'll be getting a telling off from Jean if I don't hurry up.'

'See you soon.' Clover smiled, turning her back on him to open the door. By the time she'd unlocked it, Ed had already turned and was heading back to his shop.

She shut the door behind her, and let out a sigh. Instantly she felt alone in the house. Her mum was still at work, and really, she wanted to turn and run back to Ed. Wanting to give up on her idea of a relaxing afternoon and instead sit in his shop and keep him company. Throwing her bag into the hallway, she headed upstairs. A bath was what she'd do, then maybe, she might head down to his shop to grab herself a treat before starting her film. A grin spread across her face, as she thought of the teenage crush which was happening.

Sliding down into the bubbles not long after, she grabbed her phone from the side. It had been a while since she had touched any social media but decided to start by logging into her private Facebook account; not the one she used for modelling. This one was kept for her exceedingly small circle of family and friends. Surprised to see a new friend request, she clicked on it. Edward Knight, smiled back at her and she instantly clicked accept. She wasn't long through scrolling through his page when a message popped up from him.

Took you long enough. Thought you were pretending you didn't liked me. Xx

Clover wrote and removed a variety of messages in reply to him before settling on the one she thought was appropriate.

Sorry, only just logged on. Nice to have you on my list of friends. Xx

Seeing the 3 ellipses and the phrase 'Edward is typing', Clover waited patiently.

How lucky am I? I now get to scroll through your Facebook page, delving into your deepest darkest secrets and finding those hideous photos I know are lurking on there 😊. Enjoy your bath xxx

Smiling back to herself, she closed his chat and had a quick scroll through his own page, finding only a few pictures where he'd been tagged in and others of his shop which he had uploaded. Placing her phone back on the side. Sliding down into the bath she closed her eyes and reflected on the last couple of months. She had never believed that she would be living back with her mother and doing up Hope Cottage as hers. Her thoughts were disturbed at the vibration of her phone. Rushing to grab it, secretly expecting it to be Ed, she was shocked to see an unknown local number.

'Hello?' she answered cautiously.

'Hello.' The male voice replied. 'This is Mr James from Harper and James calling for an erm... Mrs Harding.' His voice was almost a whisper as he recalled her fake name.

'Ah, Hello Mr James. This is Clover.'

'Oh good,' His voice replied, almost relieved. However, Clover noticed a sense of tension in it too.

'Is everything ok?'

'Well, there's been some development on the case you asked us to proceed with.'

'Development?' Clover quizzed. She had really hoped Rob would be civil, maybe she'd judged him incorrectly.

'Yes, and erm, well we were wondering; Mr Harper and I, if you'd like to come into the office and discuss them with us?'

'Come in? Can you not explain over the phone?

Conscious of creating any splashing noises from the bath water, she slowly stood up. Lying in the bath, didn't seem to be the most appropriate place to talk to your lawyer.

'It would be easier if you came in. I'm not sure it would be best to be discussed over the phone.'

'I see.' Was all Clover could reply, her heart began to flutter with nerves as she tried to guess what the matter could be. 'When would be best to come in?'

'Anytime really. Today?'

'Today?' Clover gasped in shock, it was nearly 3pm, she was sure their offices closed shortly. 'I don't think I'll get there in time.'

'It's no bother. We'll wait. See you shortly Mrs Harding.'

'Clover. Please, Clover is fine. See you soon.'

Ending the call, Clover threw her phone down onto the side in frustration. Everything had seemed to be going too well. Rushing through into the bedroom, she pulled out clean clothes from her wardrobe. She wondered what fuss Rob could have caused to create such an air of emergency.

Thirty-Six

Clover pulled into the nearly empty parking lot; only two cars remained, and she assumed they belonged to Mr. Harpers and Mr. James. All of the other offices around the building were shrouded in darkness, but a single light illuminated the reception desk inside. The door made a heavy thud as she closed it behind her, echoing through the empty hallways. She took a few steps forward and called out, 'Hello?'

When there was no answer, Clover felt her heart quicken in anticipation. Suddenly, a man appeared from around the corner; she had never seen him before.

'Ah Clover, pleased to meet you. I'm Mr Harper.' He extended a hand for her to shake, which she took. 'Mr James is just in his office, come this way.'

Clover followed him, down the short corridor, which she had only walked down last week. The nerves started to build within her, as the importance of both lawyers needing to attend echoed some worry.

Entering the office, Clover instantly took the seat, which was offered to her, as Mr Harper took his seat next to Mr James on the other side of the desk.

'Thank you for coming, Clover. It's really appreciated.'

'What's happened?' Clover replied, wanting to get straight to the point.

Mr James cleared his throat before beginning to answer her.

'Well, we opened a letter on your behalf today, which was sent to us in response to the files we sent to your husband.' He shuffled some papers which were lying on his desk and handed one over to Clover. 'It appears your husband is wanting to sue you.'

'Sue me?' Clover gasped at him, 'What ever for?'

'I feel that you should read the letter.'

Clover's hand trembled as she reached for the letter. She carefully unfolded it, her eyes flitting over the legal jargon until they landed on something that made her stomach twist in knots. Words like "domestic abuse," "controlling," and "financial abuse" jumped out from the page, accusing her of things she had never done. Her breath caught in her throat as she struggled to make sense of the words on the paper. 'I don't understand,' she whispered, her voice barely audible above the pounding of her heart.

'In layman's terms, he wants to sue you for all of the reasons detailed.' Mr Harper stepped into answer.

'But none of this is true. None of it.'

Clover heard Mr James let out a puff of air, in relief. 'We were hoping you'd say that. So, what we've been working on all afternoon, is a way around this. However, there is the slight issue with the article.'

'Article?' Clover quizzed. 'What article?'

'As per the letter, which was sent, it seems that your husband has threatened to go to the newspapers with a feature on your relationship and the reasons for its breakdown, if we hadn't replied by a certain time.'

'And what is that day?'

Mr Harper coughed slightly, 'It was in fact today at 12pm.'

Clover felt her stomach drop and looked down at the letter.

'This letter is dated 5 days ago?'

'We can only apologise for that, it seems it was sat amongst a pile of letters, which we only got round to looking at today.'

There were no words, Clover felt herself speechless, unknowing what to say or how to act.

'If any article is written, then we could do him for slander, unless you want to try and meet his requirements in hopes that we can delay the article.' Mr Harper explained.

'Requirements?' Clover asked, thinking she must have missed that part on the letter too.

'We got in touch with his lawyer this afternoon.' Mr James continued for him, reaching out to hand Clover another document. 'And he explained that in order for the divorce to go ahead, without any slandering, then the agreed settlement fee would be 2.5 million pounds to your husband.'

'2.5 million pounds?' Clover gasped. 'Are you mad? Are they mad? I don't have 2.5 million pounds.'

Clover caught the glance which happened between Harper and James.

'I don't.' She repeated back to them, her voice cracking and tears threatened to spill out onto the sheets in front of her. 'I really don't.'

'Look, I'm going to be perfectly honest here with you Clover. We've never dealt with anything on this scale before. We deal with petty little marriage arguments, or child custody cases. I've been on the phone all morning to other law firms who I have colleagues at, asking for their advice and what our options are.'

'And what are they?'

'There are two options really, option one is that I can try and get in touch with his solicitor tonight and ask about the article, if he's even gone to the press. It could all be a ploy. At the end of the day, if what he's saying isn't true, then what has he got to say? At least then he might be able to say when it's due to be published and hopefully we'll have time to come up with a counter offer he might be happy with. Option two would be to let the article come out, if it does and see what he has to say for himself. Then we could possibly sue him for slander.'

'Slander for what?' Clover's voice cracked once more. 'My agent ditched me weeks back, and I have no work.'

'Yes, but you could have something lined up for the future, destroying your name now could risk all possibilities for any future work, and that's the line we'll go down.'

Silence fell across the office, as Clover tried to take in everything that was offered to her.

'We'll wait for the article.' She finally decided, 'I don't want him to have any of my money, it's all tied up in the house renovation at the moment and needs to last me until I figure out what my plan for the future is.'

'Right, now that's decided. You get yourself back home. I'll plan for our next steps if there is any. Like I say, this could all be a ploy to make you pay up. But if it isn't, then I want to be ready straight away.'

Clover stood from her seat, taking in all the advice given. As she stepped out of the office and into the night air, a chill ran down her spine and she wrapped her arms tightly around herself. Climbing into her car, she paused as the dim interior light illuminated her face. In that moment, Clover longed for Ed's reassuring presence to fill the silence. She quickly retrieved her phone and dialled his number, but was met with only his voicemail. With a deep sigh, she started the engine and pulled away.

Thirty-Seven

Clover squinted at the clock, barely making out the faint blue numbers that read 9:02. Confused and disoriented, she looked around and tried to recall what had happened the night before. She remembered walking into Ed's shop. There, she found him, and briefly mentioned her trip to the solicitors, not wanting to reveal Rob's messy demands for money in lieu of divorce. She recalled Ed inviting her back for food, which led to two bottles of wine—mostly drained by Clover herself—and a sudden confession that she was falling for him. With this final memory came a rush of embarrassment as she realized her clothes from the previous night were scattered across the floor. Reaching into her jeans pocket, she pulled out her phone only to discover it had no battery life.

Deciding her primarily option would be to leave Ed's flat, she quickly got dressed, made the bed, and headed out into the kitchen. Clover quickly double checked the rooms just in case Ed hadn't gone to work for some reason but found his flat empty. All apart from a note in his handwriting, next to a small plate of freshly baked croissants.

Morning thought you might be needing breakfast. See you later xxx

Clover smiled to herself, at how thoughtful he was, but was still slightly worried about her lack of memory. Grabbing the croissant, she opened the flat door and left, making sure it was fully closed. With her luck recently, it wouldn't surprise her if she left it ajar and Ed got burgled.

Heading down the road towards her mum's house, she quickly made a detour and before she knew it, she was standing outside Ed's shop. Peering through the window, she saw Mrs Jones at the counter, no doubt filling him in on her latest aliment. She watched as he listened carefully to each word Mrs Jones said and responded with just enough wit to keep their conversation lively. His eyes twinkled with mirth while his customers basked in their easy banter. Clover knew just how much Ed meant to the village folk - they adored their conversations with him and saw him as an integral part of village life. Taking a deep breath, she pushed open the door, the bell above announcing her arrival. He glanced across to see who had come in, and when his eyes met hers, a smirk appeared across his face. Mrs Jones also looked up from their conversation, curious to see what had caught Ed's attention.

'Hello dear.' Mrs Jones, 'I was just telling Ed here, all about my arthritis.'

Clover smiled; she knew she'd guessed the topic of conversation correctly. Picking up a loaf of multi seeded bread, Mrs Jones continued telling her all about her complaints. That was the good thing about Mrs Jones, she never needed to answer, just a nod every now and again would suffice enough. She just really wanted somebody to talk to.

'Well, I must get on, jobs to do, people to see.' She finally concluded the conversation. 'I'll be seeing you both soon.'

'It's lovely seeing you again.' Ed called out.

'See you soon Mrs Jones.' Clover repeated, as she headed out of the door. Clover moved towards the counter; her loaf of bread clutched to her chest.

'Good morning.' Ed smiled at her. 'I didn't expect you to be here this morning.'

'I erm. I needed some bread.' Clover stuttered, unaware of what had come over her. She suddenly felt a like a love-struck teenager. The butterflies were doing double black flips in her stomach, and she was unable to do anything but smile at him.

A gentle smile spread across Ed's face as he leaned in closer. 'Well, you've come to the best place for bread.' His voice was smooth, almost like a melody, and Clover couldn't help but laugh along with him. He opened the counter and stepped out from behind it, moving towards her until he was standing in front of her, mere inches apart. His finger softly grazed her chin before lifting it up to meet his gaze. Her heart raced as their lips touched, each of them melting into the kiss with ease. This felt right, like these two pieces of a puzzle were finally coming together. As their mouths pulled apart, Clover felt a warmth radiating within her chest that she'd never experienced before.

Ed gave her an extra wink as he asked if she was free that night. A bright blush rose on her cheeks at the thought of what he could be planning.

'Dress warm,' he said with a mysterious glint in his eye.

'Where on earth are we going?' She smiled in anticipation as he simply replied that it was a surprise. All she knew was that she should dress warm, so whatever they were doing must involve being outdoors.

'I'll pick you up at 6pm.' Pulling her into a hug, he kissed the top of her head. 'But for now, I have a shop to run.'

'Then I guess I'll see you at 6pm.' Clover replied, pulling apart from his embrace. Picking up her loaf of bread, she headed towards the door. 'See you soon.'

'See you soon.' Ed smiled back at her, as she closed the door behind her. She wanted nothing more to turn back and spend the day with him. However conscious of acting like a clingy 16-year-old made her walk on, despite the grin that was plastered across her face.

She opened the door to her house and trudged to the kitchen, dropping her shopping bag and freshly baked loaf of bread onto the counter. Her mother had left a note by the kettle saying she had gone out shopping. She plugged in her phone and sighed, waiting for the soft bubbling of the boiling water as it turned on. A voicemail icon appeared, and she took notice, feeling a slight knot form in her stomach. Taking a deep breath, she pressed play and listened to the message from Harper and James.

'Hello Clover, this is Mr James calling from Harper and James. I just thought I'd let you know that Robs lawyer has been in touch and has given us a seven days' time frame to respond. This has put us in an advantageous position to negotiate with him. So, we're coordinating with some other lawyers of ours, so we know what action best to take and we'll let you know. I've pencilled you in for an appointment 3 days from now at 3pm to discuss what we've found. Give us a call if that doesn't suit. Thanks.'

Ending the voicemail, Clover breathed a sigh of relief. Rob was known for his hard-line stance, and it seemed that this time he was giving her a break. She glanced at her phone and opened her calendar, entering the next appointment before she turned her thoughts to her date with Ed later in the day. Her smile deepened as she thought about all the possibilities ahead.

Thirty-Eight

Clover stood in front of her mirror, watching as she put on the grey jumper dress and then pulled up her black tights. She tugged at the fabric to smooth out any wrinkles before sitting on the bed and lacing up her high-top converses. Her mind was racing; would this outfit be enough for tonight? Ed had been so careful with the words he had used - 'dress warm' - but Clover's interpretation of his message could still go either way.

She grabbed her long woollen coat and draped it over her arm, ready to put on outside once they left. After a few swipes of mascara and a quick look in the mirror, there was a knock at the door. She gave herself a pat on the back for being ready on time and opened it.

Ed stood there in front her wearing dark jeans and a grey woollen coat. His gaze swept over Clover's body, taking in every inch of her outfit. 'You look beautiful,' he said, breaking their momentary silence. It was the first time he'd ever complimented her since they met, but Clover couldn't help feeling that it was because he'd tried to always keep their relationship platonic until last night.

Mustering up all the confidence she could find, Clover smiled back at him, 'Thanks. You don't look half bad yourself.'

He suppressed a smile as she tugged her coat around her and stepped out onto the street. "Where are we going?" Clover asked, looking up at him with anticipation.

'You'll see,' he replied, lacing his fingers through hers. As they walked, Ed chattered about his day and gossiped about the happenings of their village. Soon enough they arrived at Hope Cottage, and Clover furrowed her brow in confusion.

Ed led her down the garden path past the house, across a little bridge over a babbling brook, up and over a stile into the next field. When they reached the old orchard, which had been neglected for many years, Clover stopped short in disbelief. Before them was an oasis of beauty; all weeds had been cleared away to make room for lush trees abundant with fruit. Fairy lights glowed between each tree, casting a magical light over blankets laid out on the ground with a picnic basket and wine cooler beside it.

'Oh my god Ed. This is amazing.' Clover finally broke the silence. 'When on earth did you do this?'

'I found this place not long after you started working on the house, I just saw the potential straight away and I've been clearing it over the last couple of weeks.' Ed explained. 'The trees are still in perfect condition; they just needed a bit of TLC.'

'Honestly, this is amazing. I really can't believe it.'

'Come on, I'll give you a tour.'

They strolled through the orchard, Ed's arm lightly brushing against Clover's shoulder as he shared information pointing out what each tree bore and when they'd be ready for picking. When they reached the picnic blanket, an amber glow of lanterns illuminated their faces and a bottle of chilled Prosecco filled two glasses. He passed her one, their fingertips lingering longer than necessary, before he lowered his mouth to hers in a tender kiss.

Clover nestled in the crook of Ed's arm as they stared upwards between the apple tree branches towards the stars, sipping from their second bottle of sparkling wine.

'Tell me about your last relationship,' she asked eventually, breaking the tranquil atmosphere. Ed sighed, disengaging himself from her grasp. 'Why? They're in the past with good reason.'

'Humour me.' She persisted as her fingers intertwined with his again. 'Please tell me about your last relationship.'

He sighed again and the air was filled with silence for a few seconds which felt like hours. Then he spoke.

'She was called Annie. Well Annabelle, but she always preferred Annie. We met at one of the restaurants I was working at, she was one of the customers, who had a massive complaint about her meal. I should have known then to stay away.'

'What happened?'

'At first everything. There was something about her which drew me to her. Hook, Line and Sinker, I believe the saying goes. I literally couldn't leave her alone, we dated briefly, and moved in together very quickly. Well, she moved in with me. Then things went sour quickly.'

He paused, and sat up, taking a sip of his drink. Clover sat up, crossed legged facing him, she could tell this was a difficult conversation for him and now she felt guilty for pushing him to go on.

'Look, you don't have to carry on.' Clover announced.

Ed turned to face her and picked up her hands.

'I want to.' He continued. 'When you first asked, I didn't want to, but now I've started I want you to hear it. But you have to understand, this isn't something I'm proud to talk about.'

Clover nodded, gripping his hands in reassurance.

'It all started snowballing slowly, but I didn't know until months and months down the line. She moved into mine because she said it didn't make sense us spending all our time together and having one of our empty places. It makes sense, right? So, I agreed, and within the week she'd moved in. She was only renting, which made it easier for her to move then me. The first few months were perfect, we were literally living the lover's dream. Then came the tantrums.'

'Tantrums?' Clover asked curiously.

'Tantrums. It started over simple things; she couldn't get the parking space she wanted at the supermarket. They were out of stock of her favourite wine. That sort of thing.'

'Hang on, what do you mean by tantrums?'

'Imagine a toddler, the full-blown anger when they don't get what they want. It would take hours for her to come out of them and most of the time it would be me feeling guilty. It was always my fault for some reason or another. I took too long to get ready, else the parking space would be there. I lingered too long looking in one of the aisle's, which meant somebody else took the last bottle of wine. It would mean the silent treatment until something brought her out of her moods, which generally meant me going out of my way to treat her.'

Clover didn't know how to respond, but she sounded like the devil. Ed took another sip of his drink before carrying on.

'After that, her true colours really started to show. It was almost like I couldn't do anything right at all unless I was spending money on her. I started coming home from work with presents every single day, the days I didn't, she'd shout at me that I didn't love her. She'd go about the flat slamming cupboards, doors, hitting stuff. Then the silent treatment would happen, we'd go to bed not talking and, in the morning, everything would be back to normal. I could never understand it, just could never get my head around it.'

'Did your friends and family know?'

'No. I hadn't seen them since we were together, she didn't like them, and it was easier to keep the peace with her then to see them and spend hours or days with her torturing me. Every time we were invited, I made excuse upon excuse and gave reason upon reason as to why we couldn't attend. We quickly spiralled into the relationship of doom. I dreaded going home, as I didn't know what mood she'd be in. She'd throw insults and insults at me, told me how unhappy I made her, even though I gave her everything I could. The problem was. I was stuck, she had nowhere else to go, so I couldn't just end the relationship and stop seeing her. Every time I suggested it, it's like she flipped a switch and turned nice again for a couple of weeks. It was just a never-ending circle.'

'How did it end?'

'By coming here. Finding about my dad and Katie helped me find a way to escape. Every time I visited; I just knew this was the place I needed to be. She never came here with me, which as you might imagine by now didn't go down well with her. But being here and being away from her made it easier to think, so I'd just come here more and more often for day trips. Doing nothing but driving out here with a flask of tea and sandwich. Then one day I made my mind up, I saw the shop for sale and couldn't think of anything else. It was a risk, but I just had this feeling that it was the right risk to take. I managed to get an estate agent round to my place while she was out one day, so she didn't even know the place was going up for sale. I felt awful for doing it, but I just knew that if I told her what I was doing, I'd be stuck forever. I even did it as a private sale, so there was no for sale board up outside the flat. She didn't know until the day the sale was agreed and we were a couple of weeks off from exchanging contacts. The shop was all set to go, and I lived out of the office until I found my flat. The minute contracts were exchanged, I left her with a couple of grand to find a place to rent and all my furniture from the flat. I literally left with my clothes.'

'Wow. That definitely is some story, and I'm really sorry you had to go through that.'

'It's not easy telling people. It isn't easy for a man to ever say he was bullied by a female.'

'I believe, in this day and age that stigma has gone. We all know abusers come in all shapes and sizes, and you should never be ashamed or embarrassed.' Clover reassured. 'Have you heard from her since?'

'She tried to call and text hundreds of times, I never answered, and in the end, I blocked her completely. I just couldn't have her destroying my happy place.'

'I think you did the right thing.' Clover met his gaze with a gentle smile, squeezing Ed's hand in a reassuring manner. He suddenly leaned forward and kissed her fiercely, as if a dam had burst within him, letting out all the passion he had suppressed for so long. They clung to each other, pressed together on the blanket, exploring each other with their hands until they were desperate to have more of each other. As their bodies trembled with pleasure, Ed and Clover rolled onto their backs and turned their faces up towards the starlit sky. When the heat of their lovemaking cooled, they simply lay there in awe of what had just happened between them. Even after six months in Glen Hopes, neither had found someone like this before. Clover couldn't help wondering how they both had escaped to Glen Hopes as lost souls and happened to find each other.

'I'm glad you're here.' Ed broke the silence.

'I'm glad you're here.' Clover replied, snuggling into him.

Thirty-Nine

Clover spent the next two days in a pleasant fog with Ed. They laughed at his shop, shared stories while walking around Hope Cottage, and curled up together on the sofa in his flat. But just as she was starting to forget about her appointment, her phone beeped a reminder. She glanced down and saw Harper and James' names flashing across the screen.

'What is it?' Ed asked, noticing her expression change.

'Just an appointment with the solicitors - they want to give me an update this afternoon.'

'An update?' Ed quizzed, and Clover remembered she'd yet to have told Ed about the current situation.

'Yeah, um, just seeing where we go after having no contact with Rob.' She didn't know why she found herself lying and promised herself that she would tell him everything once she knew herself this afternoon.

'I think it's pretty straight forward if there's no contact from the other party.' Ed explained, whilst filling up the baskets with freshly baked goods. 'I'm sure it's in your hands from then on. You'll be celebrating soon enough, I'm sure.'

Clover nervously smiled in response as Ed brushed off her doubts. She'd underestimated just how far Rob could take his maliciousness and was beginning to worry. She bit her lip, keeping her concerns tucked away while she answered Ed's question.

'What time's your appointment?'

'3pm, so I'll leave here about 2.30. Hopefully, I won't be long. I could pick us up a takeaway on the way back?'

'That sounds great.' He said, walking over to her and wrapping his arms around her. 'However, I've been a bit distracted over the last couple of days and am really running low on stock. Therefore, as soon as the shop is shut, I need to head over to the wholesalers, and I've got an evening of baking and proofing. I can't let the villagers down with my lack of baking.'

Clover snuggled into him, taking in every scent. Kissing the top of her head, he whispered 'So I'll see you tomorrow, I'm afraid.' Lifting her head up, she pouted at him, as a toddler would do to an adult who had just told them no.

'I could come and help when I'm done?'

'Honestly, it's fine. I'll just put the radio on and get cracking. If I'm done earlier, I'll let you know. You get back and spend some time with your mum. I'm sure she'd love a girly night in.'

'That sounds lovely actually.' Clover replied, 'I don't think she's working this evening either.'

Pushing away from her, Ed went back to restocking the shelfs, while Clover made them both a drink.

'I've been thinking.' She shouted over the noise of the coffee machine. 'About the Orchard.'

'Yeah?'

'Will you teach me what do with it all? Do you think I could sell any of it in the shop?'

'That sounds like a great idea.'

'I was thinking of getting some chickens too, so I can sell you their eggs, and whatever I grow in the greenhouse.'

Ed leaned against the counter, eyes twinkling with amusement as he teased, "Clover's little farm shop, eh?"

Clover smiled to herself, recalling the former version of herself - always having her hair and makeup done, wearing stylish clothes and big sunglasses while out. This new version of Clover was so much more genuine and truer to who she really was.

'Clover's Farm Shop.' She nodded in agreement and handed him his coffee.

Clover pulled into the car park of the solicitors, and as she shut off the engine, her mind raced with ideas for Hope Cottage. She imagined a pick your own fruit farm in the back, easily accessible from one of the lanes, and a Farm shop to hold special themed events. Once this paperwork was finalized and she had her share of their flat, she would be ready to start making those plans a reality.

Taking a few deep breaths to collect her thoughts, Clover opened her car door. As she made her way toward the entrance of Harper and James she felt a lightness fill her chest - this was it. After pushing open the door and stepping through, she noticed an unfamiliar face at reception – different from her last visit.

'Good afternoon', Clover said with a smile. 'I'm here to see Mr James – my name is Clover.'

The receptionist jerked her head up, her eyes wide with disbelief and her mouth gaping open. Clover recognized the awe— she'd been living in seclusion in Glen Peaks for weeks, but she still hadn't adjusted to the overwhelming affect her old life had on people. She sighed, repeating, 'I'm here to see Mr James,' and the receptionist snapped out of her daze, clattering at the keyboard with abrupt purpose. She flipped rapidly through pages of a giant desk planner.

'Erm. What time is your appointment?'

'3pm.' Clover responded, feeling confused herself, hoping she hadn't got the wrong appointment. Luckily, Mr James came down the corridor.

'Ah, Ms Harding. Right this way please.'
The receptionist seemed even more baffled, and Clover smiled to herself, forgetting that she had given an alternative name to begin with. Mr James must have kept it on his system.

The office seemed all too familiar, and Clover quickly took her seat opposite Mr James' desk. After the usual formalities and polite chit chat, Mr James opened her case file on his desk.

'We've been working tirelessly over the last couple of days, corresponding with everybody and anybody to see what routes we can legally take and what our options are, without causing too much of a scene.'

'And what are they?'

'Well, there's not much, I'll be honest. You have two, maybe three. Firstly, you could offer him a counteroffer. I know you said you can't afford what he's asking for, so giving him a counteroffer might play on your favour.'

'Secondly?'

'Let him go ahead with whatever he has, once we have all the evidence he has, then we'll object to everything he throws at it. It ends up in court, and the judge will decide what to do.'

Clover sighed; she didn't want either of those options. 'Did you say there was a third?'

'I did.' Mr James cleared his throat. 'The only other option, is to pay what he wants and get this over and done with.'

'What if I don't like any of those?' Clover asked, trying not to sound as obnoxious as she did.

'I'll be honest Clover, there isn't much else. Either way Rob wants money. I'm certain from talking to his solicitor that's all he wants, and he'll do whatever he will to get it.'

'What would you do?'

Mr James puffed out a breath of air. 'I'll be honest, I'd go with the counteroffer. You've said yourself you can't afford what he's asking, all you want is a divorce and the share of the flat you had with him. Would it be possible to offer him your share of the flat and see if that would suffice?'

'I need my share of the flat.' Clover explained. 'The rest of my income is tied up in the renovation of Hope Cottage, once that's done, I won't have much left at all. I need the share of the flat.'

'Then unfortunately that leaves us with option number two. The chances are whatever he has to say probably won't be much. They're all lies you've told us, so all the risk would be for you is a couple of bad weeks in the press. You could even sell your story to make a bit extra, we'll do him for slander and if our case is strong enough then you win.'

'I need to think about it. Would that be, ok? How long have we got?'

'We've got another couple of days, but I'd need your response asap, then we can get our side ready for whatever choice you make.'

Clover nodded in agreement. She wanted neither of the choices, but knew she'd have to make one of them.

Clover drove the backroads to Glen Peaks, winding through the lush expanse of rolling hills and countryside. The setting sun bathed everything it touched in a soft golden light. At a roadside pull-in, she stepped out of the car to admire the view and was brought back to memory of Ed taking her there just two months prior. A few yards away, a food truck sat on the edge of the road, its scents beckoning her to it. She ordered a cup of tea despite knowing it wouldn't measure up to her expectations. Across the street, she hopped over a stile and into a field that provided an impressive vantage point to take in Glen Peaks below. Fascinated by the beauty of it all, she sensed how blessed she felt to have come home again. Draining her cup, she returned to her car and made her way back into the village.

    Slowly, Clover drove past Ed's shop and noticed the lights still on. Pulling into the driveway of Hope Cottage, Clover's nerves heightened with each step towards the front door. She unlocked it, stepped inside, and breathed in the musty scent of plaster and dust that filled the air. Despite its newness, the house was steeped in memories: dolls pushed through hallways in pretend prams, her mother carrying laundry down the stairs, Christmas trees standing proud in a living room corner, grandparents cosied up for an evening meal. Everywhere she looked were memories that tried to a hold her there - memories that could no longer be part of her life. With a deep sense of sorrow, Clover realized that this would be the last time she'd experience such a feeling in this house. Turning back towards the door to leave, Clover felt an immense tightness in her chest as if all her breath had been stolen from her lungs. She collapsed onto the grass outside in a state of anguish and let out a flood of tears for all that Hope Cottage represented.

Forty

'I didn't hear you get in last night.' Her mother said as soon as Clover made her way downstairs that morning, wiping a tear away with the back of her hand and tucking a few renegade hairs behind an ear. Secretly she was pleased that she didn't mention the proposed movie night they were both supposed to have had. Clover had arrived home after midnight, exhaustion heavy on her shoulders and red-rimmed eyes betraying the tears she had shed over the past few hours. The living room was dark except for the glow of the television and her mother who lay asleep on the sofa, snoring lightly and cocooned in a worn blanket from last winter. Careful not to wake her, Clover tip-toed up to her bedroom, yawning as she got ready for bed.

'I didn't want to wake you,' She replied softly as she accepted the cup of coffee which had been made for her. 'Sorry I was late back; we definitely need a night in together.' She smiled weakly at her mother, hoping that she wouldn't see the dread that seemed to be sitting like a stone at the bottom of her stomach. Recently she'd spent so much time either with Ed or at Hope Cottage, she hadn't found the opportunity to update her mother on any of the recent events regarding his impending divorce. To be honest, she now felt that she'd left her mum out of the loop completely, and they'd just been passing ships over the last few weeks.

'We definitely do,' Her mum replied, 'However, I'll be late for work if I don't get a move on. We'll arrange one soon, yeah?'

Clover felt her breath catch as her mother's figure receded out the kitchen door. Anxiety had been gnawing away at her since leaving the solicitor's office the night before, a feeling she was unaccustomed to. As she swallowed back tears and dumped the remaining contents of her coffee into the sink, Clover hastily decided to visit Ed, looking for an escape from the painful emotions swirling inside her.

A pleasant spring day greeted her outside, with beams of sunlight washing away some of her sorrows. However, upon entering Ed's shop, those feelings returned with renewed intensity. There he was, bent over the counter buried in a newspaper.

'Good morning.' She said as cheerfully as she could manage.

'Good morning?' Ed replied, a hint of sarcasm in his voice as he looked up from the paper. 'I can't believe it, you're just like her.'

'Who?' Clover stammered, as she watched Ed come from behind the counter, holding what he was reading.

'Her. Annie.' He stomped towards the door, flipping the sign to closed, then thrust a newspaper into Clover's hands, and instantly her stomach dropped.

THE HIDDEN SIDE TO CLOVER. ALL REVEALED.

Taking the paper, she scanned the page as highlighted words jumped out of the page – *'Narcist', 'Controlling', 'Fake', 'Emotional Abuse.'*

Pictures of her and Rob on nights out were splattered across the page, with captions underneath them, she read one of them; *'Clover playing happy couples, just hours before they went back to their flat, where Rob suffered hours of verbal abuse from her.'*

Clover felt the air rush out of her lungs like she'd been punched in the gut. Her heart raced and her hands trembled as Ed continued,

'I thought you were different. But this, this is almost like reading an article about Annie and me.' She opened her mouth to protest but it felt like there was a lump stuck in her throat.

'No,' she whispered hoarsely, tears welling up in her eyes. 'It's all lies.'

'And that's exactly what Annie would have said. I'd like you to leave.' Ed's voice was cold and distant as he motioned for the door with an outstretched arm, and she felt her feet move involuntarily in its direction. The door slamming behind her.

Just as Clover wiped away her tears, a strange male voice called out to her. The sudden flash of light blinded her momentarily, and through watery eyes she saw the figure of a photographer, his camera pointed toward her expression of distress. 'Have you read the papers yet?' He continued, as Clover turned to walk away. Flash. Flash. Flash. More cameras at every point catching her every moment.

'Clover, over here!' Voices shouted from across the street, and Clover's gut churned with fear. She quickly crumpled up the paper in her hand and sprinted back towards her mother's house. The sound of snapping cameras and shouted questions followed her as she struggled to find her keys. Finally, she was able to push open the door, slam it shut behind her, and collapse on the floor. The sound of banging against the wood made her jump, so she scrambled up the stairs and dived under the covers.

Hours later she heard her mum climbing up the steps and pushing open the door to her room.

'Clover?' she whispered into the dark, but Clover stayed silent and unmoving until night had fallen, and all was still.

Forty-One

Clover lay in bed, exhausted from the sleepless night but still jolting awake at the soft knock on her bedroom door. 'Clover are you awake?' her mother's voice asked gently. Clover didn't answer, unable to face what had been written about her or discuss it with her mum. The door creaked open, and she quickly closed her eyes, keeping them shut until she heard the click of the handle when it was pulled closed again.

She could hear her mother talking on the phone out on the landing. 'Hi Ed, it's me, Emma. I'm worried about Clover,' she said. Silence followed while Clover assumed Ed was responding on the other end. Her stomach churned as she wondered what he was saying.

'Oh, I see.' Her mother finally replied. 'I'm just really worried about her. She never answered any of my messages yesterday and was in bed when I got back and is still in bed now.'

More silence continued. It was torture not being able to hear what was happening on the other side.

'Of course, I've tried to talk to her, but she's sleeping, and I need to go to work soon.'

Clover wished she could get up. To be the strong woman everyone thought she was, but her body was suddenly too heavy to move.

'Right, well thanks for all your help.' Her mother sounded annoyed. 'Bye Ed.'

Another knock on the door came, and her mother entered. Clover felt her bed creak from the additional weight and Clover curled into a ball and squeezed her eyes shut.

'Clover honey are you ok?' her mother asked with concern in her voice. Silence was her only reply. 'I spoke to Ed; he said I needed to talk to you.' But still, no words came out of Clover's mouth. She wanted to desperately speak up, to tell her mother about the divorce, the threats from Rob, the article, and about how Ed believes she is no longer who he thinks she is. Yet, it seemed impossible for her to find the courage to share all this with her mother.

Resignation filled the room as her mother sighed and rose from the bed. The creaking of the old floorboards signalled that she was being left alone again.

'I've got to go to work.' Her mother said. 'Call me anytime you need me.'

The door closed behind her. Clover listened to the everyday movements happening downstairs in the kitchen, as her mother prepared herself for her day ahead.

She pondered how she'd evaded the paparazzi who had hounded her like prey. Or how she'd not heard about the newspaper report. Surely someone who knew her would have shown her.

Hearing her mother leave the house, it took another hour before Clover finally pulled herself from her bed. Padding along the landing to the bathroom, her legs felt weak but heavy at the same time. The similar feeling as when she had a bad case of Flu a couple of years previously. Her mouth was dry from not drinking or talking for the last 24 hours. Pulling on her dressing gown, which was hung on the back of the bedroom door, she made her way down the stairs. She didn't have a clue where her phone was, and ultimately didn't want to know. Wherever it was, it would no doubt be filled with missed calls or messages from the local press. Making herself a cup of tea, she went into the living room, lay down on the sofa and pulled a blanket over her. Laying still, she tried to focus on her senses, how she'd been taught to keep herself calm in previous situations. The pit of her stomach was still full to the brim with anxiety, making her feel suffocated and unable to concentrate or breathe.

Starting with her breathing, she concentrated on breathing in through her nose and out her mouth in a slow and relaxed manor. Regulating it. Staying still, she carried on breathing in through her nose and out of her mouth, until she finally felt that she could begin to think again. She was just about to sit up and drink her tea, when a knock on the door undid everything, she'd just worked hard on. Sending her spiralling back into a panicked state. Staying still, she dared herself not to move just in case whoever had just knocked knew she was there. The knock came again, this time followed by a voice she had come to recognise all too much.

'Clover. I know you're in there.' Ed called through the letterbox.

Clover held her breath and fought back the tears that threatened to come.

'Clover. Just open the door.' He called again. 'Let me in.'

No matter how much she longed to have Ed come in and tell her how it would be ok, and to have him wrap his arms around her. She knew that it just wouldn't happen. The hurt she saw in his face just yesterday morning was etched on her mind, and she couldn't bear to face it again. Couldn't bear to hear him compare her to his ex. The ex who had broken him.

The knocking and calling had stopped shortly after. Which Clover assumed meant that he had left. Laying still, she realised she'd have to at some point decide what to do. How far would Rob go to get the money he so much demanded? Her lawyers had already suggested to pay him before the article was released to protect her reputation. But now that all seemed pointless. Knowing she'd have to talk to the only people who had any contact with Rob, she raced upstairs and quickly washed and changed her clothes. Pulling a cap over her unwashed hair, she left through the back door, quickly racing through the back alleyways to get to her car before anyone could spot her.

Forty-Two

Clover squealed into the carpark, skidding to a stop in the first available space. She raced towards the door of Harper and James, yanking it open with both hands and stepped inside in a hurried frenzy. The receptionist looked up from her desk, eyes widening for an instant before she gracefully directed Clover through to Mr James' office.

'Can you get Mrs Harding a cup of coffee please Emily?' Mr James asked the receptionist who had shown her to his office. 'Oh, and pop out to the bakers and grab some sandwiches too if you don't mind.'

'Did anyone follow you?' He asked Clover, the minute the office door had closed.

'I don't think so. ' Clover swallowed, 'I don't think anyone saw me leave anyway.'

'Good. Luckily, nobody seems to know we're representing you.' He seemed pleased. 'Yet.'

'What do I do?' She begged, trying to keep the sobs from escaping. 'It's all lies. All of it.'

'Look, as you know we've never dealt with something like this on this scale before. But at the end of the day, we need to look at it from a messy divorce point of view. Trust me, we've dealt with plenty of them. Where one party or the other is trying to gain a bigger financial gain through lies and slander.'

'But what do I do?' Clover begged again. 'What would you do?'

'As we spoke the other day, one of your options has already gone out of the window. It's too late to pay Rob off before anything has been released. Which means, we now have two options. The first option is to fight this, take him to court for slander. He'll be asked to provide evidence of his accusations. You'll be asked to provide counterevidence and it will be battled out against the court. The other option, is pay him what he wants, get the divorce filed and accept whatever damages to your reputation and career this has had.'

'Either way, I loose and he wins.'

'What makes you say that?'

'To fund the court fees, I would need to sell Hope Cottage. To pay him off, I'd have to sell Hope Cottage. Either way it will need to be sold, and that's all I've wanted for the last couple of months.'

'That maybe. However, if we went to court and you could prove that everything, he's saying is false. Then he would owe you. I reckon we could sue him for a lot.'

The door opened and Emily came in carrying take-away coffees and a box full of a variety of sandwiches and pastries.

'Just place it down over there please.' Mr James indicated to the top of a filing cabinet.

'Can I have a quick word with you?' Emily almost whispered in their direction. 'Outside.'

'Of course.' Mr James replied, rising from his seat to follow Emily into the corridor. Pulling the door to slightly so that it was still ajar.

Clover stood and headed over to where Emily had placed the food and drinks, managing to hear snippets of the conversation outside of the room.

'Another article.' Emily whispered. The rustling of papers outside. Mr James mumbled something else which Clover couldn't quite catch. Her heart was beating faster than ever at the thought of what Rob could have written now.

'Thank you for letting me know.' Mr James said aloud, as he pushed the office door open. Clover jumped slightly, before picking up the coffee and heading back to his desk.

'Well, there seems to be an unexpected turn of events.' Mr James sighed as he eased himself into his chair, unfolding the newspaper which was in his hand. 'It looks like Rob has someone else to back his side of the story.'

'Oh god.' Clover exclaimed, 'Who is it?'

Mr James held up the paper, the headline in bold, standing out from anything else.

GAME CLOVER FOR THE UK'S LUCKILEST MODEL. BEST FRIEND RACHEL REVEALS ALL LATEST REVELATIONS.

'Do you want to read it?'

Clover shook her head, 'You do it.' Sipping her drink, she stayed silent the few short minutes it took Mr James to scan the page.

'I'll be honest, there's not much new that hasn't been said in the interview Rob did. It's mainly just backing up what he said. There are a few extra parts about you being controlling and demanding on set. A few bits about always having to have your own way.' He stopped and looked up at Clover, who was staring back in disbelief.

'It's all lies.' Clover repeated, 'All of it, lies. She's only doing it because he's telling her to.'

'So, what do you want to do?'

Clover remained silent while she thought. Personally, she'd love nothing more than to run away from all of this. Ed by her side and to start again, somewhere where she wasn't known.

'The way I see it,' Mr James continued, 'You either sell Hope Cottage, give Rob his money and hear nothing else, whilst potentially being bankrupt. Or you don't give Rob the money, sell Hope Cottage and use the money for the case. If, and I mean if, everything you say about these accusations being a lie is true, then not only will you keep the money. You will gain financially too. Now Rachel has stepped up, we can sue her too for slander while we're at it. Which to me, means a double win.'

Clover thought briefly, as Mr James flicked through the newspaper in front of him.

'We'll fight it.' She finally decided. 'What do you need me to do?'

'For now, not a lot. It's not going to be a quick process I'm afraid, and we'll easily be looking at 6-8 months before any court date is set. However, what that time does give us, is time to gather evidence against them. It also gives you time to sell Hope Cottage and raise the funds. Of course, we will be more than happy to help you out with that side of things too. You'll just need to sort the estate agent.'

'Any recommendations?' Clover sighed. As quickly as Mr James' brain was going into overdrive, hers seemed to be drowning.

'I tell you what, I'll give some of the local estate agents a call for you. For now, go home, get some rest and either I'll be in touch or the estate agent.'

Clover nodded, and her eyes welled up at his kindness. For too many times this week already, she had no words to say. Gathering her car keys, she whispered a thank you and left the office. Feeling lost with what to do with herself, she climbed into the car. The drive to

Glen Peaks happened on complete autopilot, and before she knew it, she was pulling into the driveway of Hope Cottage. Surprised that there were no paparazzi hanging around, she quickly exited the car and ran through the gardens, over the bridge and into the orchard. This place was still a secret, she was sure her mum had even forgotten about this place. Walking through it, she was amazed that already fruit was beginning to grow, it was shame she had to give this up. A dream just months ago she didn't even know existed. Slumping down against one of the tree trunks. Memories of how she used to sit on the grass as child, pulling up strands of grass, or daisies came to her mind. Even trying to find another four-leaf clover, which her mum so famously found the day before she was born. *I doubt they'll be a four-leaf clover here* she thought to herself as a single tear fell down her face.

A shadow looming over her, caught her attention and she was shocked to find Ed standing there. Jumping up to her feet, they came face to face.

'I knew I'd find you here. I was so worried about you...' Ed spoke, his words heavy with regret. Clover felt a wave of confusion wash over her and she desperately wanted to get away from him. She shuddered at the thought of the next eight months, not wanting to bear any more of Ed's disapproving stares.

'Clover, please!' he pleaded, an edge in his voice. 'Don't go. Don't leave me like this!'

The desperation in his voice made her stop dead in her tracks. Taking a deep breath, she slowly turned around to face him.

'What do you want?' her voice was strained. 'To remind me how I deceived you? To remind me how much like Annie I am and how much you are the victim in all of this?'

'I...' Ed began, but before he could continue Clover found herself unable to control what came next.

'No, Ed, no.' she began, her voice growing louder with anger. 'Remember when you first met me? You were different than anyone else. I'll tell you why were different, and it's because you didn't read the newspapers. You didn't believe the press. Remember how you said, all those months ago that you wanted to hear my story, not the one they wrote? Well guess what, you're not that person after all. Because at the end of the day, you believed them. You believed them, even though you know I'm not like anything they said.' Turning to walk away again, he called her back.

'Clover, wait, I can explain.'

'No, you can't. Over the last couple of days my life has turned completely the wrong way round. I have people out there, out to get me. To ruin my name, my reputation, and any chance of me getting a job. They want more money from me than I can ever imagine owning, and the one person I thought knew me and wouldn't believe the lies, didn't. So no, you don't get to explain. The next eight months are going to be hard, and I cannot have you around judging me, or me not knowing whether you believe me or them. I can't do in it.'

The tears flowed heavier than tears have ever flowed before. Clover turned on her heel and ran as great big sobs emitted from her chest. There was no looking back, the only way was forward and somehow, she had to help herself out of this mess she'd found herself in. She had to do it alone.

Climbing into her car, she raced back to her mother's house, where she packed everything, she owned and piled it into her car. Back in the house, she sat down with paper and pen and wrote her mum a letter. A letter explaining everything that had been happened and everything that was to come. Without a doubt her mum would be on her side, which was something that she knew for sure. However right now, she couldn't face the worry and the sympathy that would come with it if she told her face to face.

I just need to get away for a while, to sort everything out. I'll be in touch soon.

Clover ended the letter, folded it up and left it by the kettle. Walking back through the house, she spotted her phone on the side, no doubt out of battery now. She'd buy a new one, she thought to herself, as she walked out of the door, climbed into the car and drove out of Glen Peaks.

Forty-Three

6 Months Later

Clover peered out at the magnificent waves that crashed against the jagged rocks on the beach. The spumes of salty seawater intermittently sprayed into her face, and she breathed in the heavy scent of fresh air, feeling invigorated by it all. Luckily, before leaving Glen Peaks, she had reached out to a very old friend she'd met years before. This friend knew she was unlike anything which was portrayed, and so he offered her sanctuary in the form of an old holiday home situated on its own secluded beach in Cornwall. Only one other neighbour resided nearby: an elderly couple in their 80s who kept to themselves. The sounds of the sea crashing onto the shore and the gentle roar of the ocean made her days peaceful as she spent time healing herself. Her days consisted of reading endless books, strolling down along the pristine sand beach, collecting shells, and cooking food from fresh ingredients that she got from a local market. If anything, it had done nothing but good to have so much time alone with nature and her thoughts.

Mr James had kept her updated on everything that was going on and even made his way down to her a couple of times to go through some evidence with her. He'd consulted with other colleagues, and he was positive that their side of the case was more than strong enough to win.

Hope Cottage had also sold within days of it being on the market. The small renovations which they had done, alongside tidying the garden and the orchards up made it more appealing and managed to fetch a nice tidy sum to cover the court fees. For the first time in a while, Clover felt that live was a lot more positive. The hearing was tomorrow, which meant Clover had to goodbye to the place she'd temporarily called home and head over to a hotel where she would stand in court tomorrow to face her case.

Mr James has assumed it would# take no more than three days at the most to go through the evidence. However, it could be pushed to five depending on Rob's solicitors and how ruthless they were.

Taking one last look at what had become her private oasis, she turned back and headed to her already packed car. Her new neighbours came out to wish her the best of luck and she promised that she'd keep in touch. Climbing into her car, she turned on the ignition and for the first time in what seemed like forever, she headed off.

Forty-Four

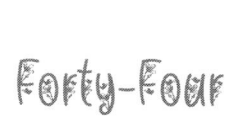

The panelled wood room, which Clover now found herself in portrayed itself as the typical court room you often saw in TVs. Mr James sat next to her, as she tried to not adjust the suit, she'd brought herself. After living in casual wear, mainly consisting of leggings and hoodies for the last six months, the suit was proving to be restricting and claustrophobic. Her palms felt sweaty, as she watched Mr James shuffle through the pile of papers which he'd brought with him, separating them into three neat piles. The room was full of people shuffling in and out of the room, most of them sitting behind her as spectators. Clover kept her face forward, refusing to look behind and equally avoiding Rob who was sat adjacent to her on the next desk with his attorney. Suddenly the side door to the room opened, and everybody stood as the judge entered and took her place overlooking the room.

'Good morning, everyone.' She greeted the room and went ahead with her formalities before bringing out the jury. Clover couldn't help but wonder how the twelve people who now stood at the side of the room, would decide the fate her life would next lead. Despite them vowing that they would be the middle ground. The neutral party. All it would take, is a considerable proportion of them to be more of Robs followers than hers. Mr James looked at her, as if he knew just what she was thinking and gave her a reassuring smile.

'Can we please go ahead with the opening statements.' The judge announced. Mr James grabbed the first piece of paper from pile one and entered the podium which was placed between both her team and robs.

'Good morning.' Mr James spoke, loud and confident to the room, but facing the jury. 'I am here representing the claimant. Mrs Clover Taylor. You may recognise Clover Taylor, as a face you grew up with. The woman who was often on the front pages of magazines or billboards. For years, she has been that face which every household knew. One of Britain's most well-respected models whose name was associated with success. Today her name is associated with a lie. A false statement uttered by her former husband. The defendant Robert Taylor. This statement as falsely cast Clover as a villain. A woman who would violently abuse a man. A woman who would use her powers against him. Controlling him and causing mental distress. This is a defamation case. It's a case about how devastating words can be when they are false and uttered publicly. Words that can destroy your name and your reputation. Under the law, a person who makes a false statement about someone else can be held responsible for the harm that results from that falsehood. That's because words matter. It paints a picture of what we know, or what we think we know. And because of that words cause irreparable harm to a person's reputation. A reputation which Clover has worked hard to build. A reputation which like Clover her career depends on. It decides who will want to work with her. Who wants her to be modelling their next range of clothes, or whether a company wants her to represent them. When this is the case, that harm can be particularly devastating. This is a case about Robert Taylors words on Clover Taylor. Specifically words he opted to post in the national newspapers just a few months previously. The Evidence is clearly shown on the screens in front of you.'

Clover looked up as the newspaper article was clearly displayed on the screen for all to see. Specific words and sentences were highlighted and enlarged for all to see. She messed with the pen laid out in front of her, as Mr James continued to tell the story of her life for the last eight months. Trying to persuade the jury that she was in the wrong. As he continued, she silently prayed that that they really would believe him. They didn't quite yet know if Rob had any hidden secrets he had yet to reveal.

'So, for the duration of this case.' Mr James continued. 'I want you to look upon the evidence from both sides. Disregarding them as public figures, but only seeing them for the individuals that they are and the evidence which is presented before you.'

Mr James gathered up his papers and made his way back to the desk which Clover was sat at. He looked quite smug with himself as he sat down. Robs lawyer than took to the podium, addressing the court just as Mr James had done. This time defending Rob and trying to persuade them not to believe any evidence which is bought against Rob in the hearing.

At this point, Clover switched off completely, she had already heard everything which they were saying about her. How manipulative and controlling she was. How throughout the whole relationship, her coercive behaviour had damaged Rob. She couldn't hear it again, so took her the notepad she had brought with her and instead started to doodle a variety of flowers all over it.

The rest of the day was spent watching a private battle happen between both sides. A constant back and forth of Clovers evidence Vs Robs. Clover was thoroughly impressed how quickly Mr James was to react to any evidence Robs team brought forward. He had cross examined every single piece of evidence and was prepared for every situation that could rise. By the end of the first day, Clover was mentally exhausted and all she'd done for the day was sit and listen. Tomorrow she would have to sit and listen to witnesses and Rob, as he took to the stand to protest his case. Today, she thought to herself, was probably the easier day of what was to come.

'You did great.' Mr James broke her thought as they left the court room.

'I think you'll find; you did great.' Clover smiled at him weakly. 'You deserve a drink tonight!'

'Not tonight. I've got this to go through tonight.' He replied, holding up the case folder he carried around with him.

'Again?'

'I just want to go through and double check everything. Preparation is the key. However, I think you need to go back to your hotel and have a drink. Get an early night. I'll get a drink when this is all over.'

'Good Plan.' Clover replied, they'd reached the waiting taxi's and they both headed to separate ones. 'I'll see you in the morning.'

Clover's heels clicked against the marble flooring as she walked across the hotel foyer, her eyes scanning the lavish decor. Just as she reached for the door handle to the corridors leading to the rooms, a nervous receptionist called out her name. Clover turned around to see the petite woman waving her arm frantically.

'I was asked to give you this when you came back.' The receptionist stuttered, holding out a small package wrapped in plain brown paper.

Clover smiled softly and couldn't help but feel curious about what could be inside. She took the package from the receptionist's hand and felt its weight. She gave it a shake, but no sound came from within.

'Thank you,' she said before turning around and walking away. As she continued on towards the room, she couldn't keep herself from glancing at the mysterious package.

Back in her room, Clover tore off the paper revealing 'The Lucky Clover' book Ed was reading back in Glen Peaks. She'd left her copy back at her mother's house. Turning it over, she saw one of the pages folded over. Opening the book on that page, a necklace with a four-leaf clover pressed into a clear disc fell out. Ed had highlighted a passage and a post-it note stuck to the page read.

I found this the day you left Hope Cottage. I had it pressed and made into this necklace for you. Ed xxx

Clover smiled to herself, as she examined the necklace. Glancing back at the book, she read the highlighted passage.

Bad luck cannot be eradicated from one's life completely. It is often said that when the lucky one experiences bad luck, all that bad luck will prevail. All it will take is for the lucky one to find another four-leaf clover and good luck will be restored.

If only this fairy tale talk was real, Clover thought to herself, as she fastened the necklace around her neck. Besides, she didn't find the clover, Ed did. Therefore, if any luck was going anyone's way, then it would indeed be Ed's.

Her hand instinctively slid to the bedside table, where she had left her new phone. She frowned when she was reminded that her Ed's number wasn't saved in any of her contacts anymore. She thought about the many times she had wanted to reach out over the past few months, but had kept herself from doing it because she didn't have his number. Now, after receiving an unexpected gift from Ed, she wanted nothing more than to call him and thank him for it.

She flopped down onto her bed and grabbed the book he had sent her from off her nightstand. Opening it to the first page, she decided she might as well spend the rest of her evening reading it.

Forty-Five

Clover arrived at the courthouse early the next day, her steps echoing in the empty hallways. She stepped into the private waiting room and saw Mr James studying a document, deep in thought.

'Good morning.' She smiled joyfully as she entered the room, Mr James had already made her a coffee and handed it to her.

'Good morning, Clover.' He eyed her suspiciously. 'I take it you slept well?'

'The best I've slept in ages. Are you all ready for today?'

'As ready as I ever will be. Unless they throw a curveball our way which we're not expecting.'

'I'm sure it will be just fine. Shall we?' Clover flashed a comforting smile at Mr James as she gestured to the door leading into the courtroom. He hastily grabbed his folder, gripping it tighter against his chest than usual as he followed her. His brows furrowed in confusion as he followed the Clover who now seemed to ooze confidence.

Sitting down at the tables which they'd sat at just the day previously, Mr James looked around and saw that Rob and his team hadn't arrived yet.

'Are you quite alright?' He leaned over to Clover and whispered.

'Absolutely.' She grinned back, and pulled out the necklace which was tucked down the top of her dress. 'I have my lucky Clover with me.'

Before the flabbergasted Mr James could reply, the hustle and bustle of Rob and his team making their presence known interrupted the silence. Rachel; Rob's new bit on the side, was leaning over the viewing barrier, shouting his name like a devoted fan would. Rob clearly not impressed, blanked her completely and followed his team to their side of the room, before demanding one of them return to the foyer to bring him a decaf coffee made with oat milk. If there was any demonstration of the person that Rob really was, then his colours were well and truly beginning to show. He glanced back at Clover, who hadn't noticed their arrival, or if she had wasn't fazed by them at all. Instead, she was gazing lovingly at the necklace which was still in her hand. Luck, Mr James thought to himself, was something he desperately needed today.

The morning went by just as slowly as the day previously, with Clover mainly doodling over the pad of paper in front her. Mr James held strong when presenting his evidence and had brought up a few points which Rob had failed to declare in his defence. Meaning the opposing team were quite often left stuttering and casting worrying looks across to Rob, who fended them off with shrugged shoulders. Which too in turn meant some worrying and unsure looks from the judge and the jury too.

'I think we'll break for lunch.' The judge announced to the room. 'We'll be back in an hour.'

'All rise.' Was shouted across the room, to signify that the Judge was leaving, and in turn the rest of the court could follow her.

'What have you got lunch?' Clover whispered to Mr James, as they made their way out of the room.

'Erm, a cheese sandwich.' He replied, trying to balance his folder, whilst opening the door for Clover.

'There's a nice sandwich shop across the road, come on I'll treat you for dinner.'

Before Mr James had chance to reply, Clover bounded down the corridor, leaving him no other option but to leave his cheese sandwich behind and follow Clover.

'How do you think it's going?' Clover said after her first mouth full of her sandwich.

'I think it's going really well.' Mr James replied, 'Our case definitely seems stronger than theirs, however we do have this afternoon of their evidence.'

'Yes, it'll be interesting to see what they have. Considering there were a few instances where his team weren't even aware of some of the bits you raised,'

Mr James swallowed his last mouthful. being quite surprised that Clover had been paying attention in court. He had looked over multiple times to see her page filled with a whole page of doodled flowers.

'We'll have to start heading back.' Mr James pushed his empty plate to the side and looked at his watch.

Clover finished the rest of her coffee and stood up. 'I'll pay.'

Clover and Mr James pushed open the heavy wooden doors to the court, their footsteps echoing through the marble-tiled corridors. They slowed as they passed a room with its door slightly ajar, catching snippets of conversation from inside.

"I can't believe you didn't tell us about anything her poxy lawyer brought up this morning!" Rob's lawyer hissed, and Clover saw Mr James flush slightly under his use of the name.

'Ah, nonsense.' Rob casually replied. Clover pictured him leaning back on his chair brushing anything his lawyer said away. 'We'll win this. You just need to do what you do best.'

'And to do that.' His lawyer continued through gritted teeth. 'I need you to tell me exactly everything you know and not make me look like a fool.'

Mr James quickly pulled Clover away as they heard footsteps moving in the room. Rushing quickly, they entered their waiting room and closed the door.

'Well, that was certainly interesting.' Clover grinned.
'Yes, it definitely was. I just hope he doesn't use his frustrations with Rob to play dirty. Trust me it happens.'

Mr James sat down at the desk and started rereading all his papers again. If anything, Mr James certainly was meticulous. Clover took the seat next to him and pulled out her phone. It was strange really; she didn't really have any use for her phone no more. Since buying a new one, she hadn't reinstalled the social media apps that used to take up all her time. Opening the email app, she quickly scrolled through. Just a year previously her inbox used to be full of people wanting her. Whether it was old friends catching up, or job offers, there was always something to reply to. Now it was filled with offers for discounts at some of the website she used to shop at. The door adjourning the court room opened and one of the assistants popped their head around, informing them that the case was ready to start again. Clover turned her phone onto silent and placed it back into her bag.

'Let's go.' Mr James stood, gathering his papers, before following the assistant out of the room. Clover quickly followed behind. 'This will be interesting.' He said, as they entered the court room and too their seats. Taking a quick glance at Rob and his team it seemed from their faces that all may not be as rosy on their side.

Forty-Six

Clover pushed open the doors of the hotel, a grin plastered across her face. They had just been informed that tomorrow would be the last day in court. Unless any new evidence became known, which Mr James was certain there wouldn't be.

'Excuse me Miss.' The receptionist called as she walked past. Clover made her way over. 'There's somebody who would like to see you in the restaurant. He's been waiting for the last thirty minutes and asked me to let you know when you came in.'

'Who is it?' Clover whispered curiously.

'I'm not sure.' The receptionist looked down at the notepad, where she'd scribbled down her notes. 'Nobody took his name.'

Clover looked cautiously towards the entrance to the restaurant. An anxious feeling washed over her, as she had visions of paparazzi wanting to sell her story for her. Or worse, Rob wanting to negotiate a private deal.

Clover took a deep breath, squared her shoulders, and walked towards the entrance of the restaurant. Clover paused at the entrance of the restaurant, scanning the guests for any familiar faces. Her heart leapt as her eyes landed on the figure across the room. He had his back to her, but she'd know him anywhere. She watched as he slowly turned around and their eyes locked. She was momentarily taken aback by his handsome features, struggling to breathe. He smiled and waved her over, and against her better judgement, she felt her body moving towards him of its own accord. Suddenly, all the pain of being apart after six months rushed back - but still, there was no denying the warmth in her heart.

He stood, as she reached the table. 'Hi.' He smiled shyly. 'I'm glad you came.'

'What are you doing here?' Clover gasped. 'Why are you here?'

Ed's smile fell from his face slightly, but he managed to fix it before answering. Clover couldn't quite help but feel he was hoping for a better welcome.

'I just wanted to see how you were doing. And to see if you got the book, I left last night.'

Clover looked down at the necklace which she was still wearing from this morning. A clear sign that she had indeed received the book and the necklace that came with it.

'I did, thank you.' She replied. Her answer short but not quite sure why. 'Look, I better be going.'

'Will you stay and eat with me?' Ed interrupted her, before she had time to finish what she was saying. She eyed him cautiously.

'Please?' he pleaded.

Clover's mouth curved into a hesitant smile, and she nodded her agreement. Ed pulled out a chair for her, which she took before picking up the menu. As she glanced around, Clover noticed the bottle of wine already on the table was the same one they had often shared back in Glen Peaks. Ed didn't even ask her if she wanted some; he simply poured her a glass, filling it nearly to the brim.

'Cheers.' He said, holding up his glass and Clover clinked her glasses against his.

'Clover.' Ed started, and Clover tried to push the butterflies back to the pit of her stomach, as they fluttered the way he said her name. 'I just need to say I'm sorry.'

Clover glared at him and picked up the menu. 'Are we just having mains?' She questioned, trying to avoid the topic of conversation she didn't want to have.

'I'm sorry Clover.' Ed said again, this time reaching over to her hand, which she managed to quickly withdraw before any energy could be passed between them.

'Let's order, shall we?' She again pushed the topic of conversation to be changed.

'Clov..' Ed pressed, but Clover stopped him before he could continue.

'Look Ed, just stop, ok?' Her breathing was heavy, as she tried to stop any form of emotion from tumbling out. 'That was six months ago, we've both moved on. You've come here for God knows what reason and have asked me to eat with you. I've said yes as it's better than sitting alone in the hotel room and trust me I've been alone a lot the six months so it's not something I'm not used to. Let's just order and eat yeah?'

Ed looked hurt, and Clover felt the lump in her throat grow bigger as she watched the false smile hide every emotion he was fighting.

'Okay then.' He smiled, as he took a sip of the wine. 'The steak sounds good. I had a quick look while I was waiting.'

'Super. I think I'll go for the carbonara.' Clover waved over one of the waiters and they both gave their order.

'So, how do you think the court case is going?' Ed asked, trying his hardest to make small talk.

Clover filled him in on the latest developments and how tomorrow would be the last day and then a decision would be made.

'Mr James seems very positive it will all go in our favour.' She smiled, draining the last drop of her wine, as Ed refilled it up. 'In fact, I've never seen him look this cheery since I've known him. No doubt it will do with the big fat cheque which will land on his doorstep if we win.'

The evening went on, as if they were old friends catching up. Clover was pleased, as at the start of the evening she felt that it was going to be upsetting for both. Ed told her tales of some of the regulars back in Glen Peaks, making her laugh doing impressions of some of them.

'The best was, Jack decided he wanted to get some Chickens.' Ed carried on with one of the tales from Glen Peaks. 'Well, he didn't think to fence them in, and the next day they were running down the middle of the high street. Chickens everywhere. It took the whole village to round them up.'

Clover had tears in her eyes from laughing so much and her cheeks ached. Something she hadn't felt she had experienced for a very long time. It also made her miss the village in a way that made her heart ache.

'So, what's next for Clover after tomorrow?' He quizzed.

'Ah I don't know. I think I'll head off for a very long holiday. Well, that's if I win. If I don't, then there definitely won't be a holiday.' She smiled sadly. 'There won't be much. But we must think positive right?'

'Right.' Ed agreed, smiling back. He so desperately wanted to reach over. Take her hand and reassure her that no matter what, she didn't need to worry. She still had him. But he couldn't.

'Look at the time.' Clover glanced at her phone. 'I really had better get going, Ed. But thanks for coming and thanks for the book and necklace.'

Ed stood, as Clover pushed herself back from the table. 'It's really no problem at all. I hope it all goes well tomorrow.'

'Fingers crossed, eh?' Clover slung her bag of her shoulder. 'Bye Ed.'

'Bye Clover.' Ed replied sadly, as he watched her turn and head out of the restaurant. Sliding down back into his seat, he waved the waiter over and ordered another drink.

Forty-Seven

The ringing of her phone made Clover's eyes fly open. She'd barely registered the number flashing on the screen of her mobile. Instead, she swiped up to answer it.

'Hello?'

'Clover, where are you?' A flustered Mr James at the end of the phone replied. Quickly pulling the phone away from her face, she looked at the time. How she'd slept through her alarm she would never know, but she needed to be at the court in twenty minutes.

'Just running late.' Clover replied, returning the phone back to her ear. She hoped she sounded casual enough to be believable. 'Be there in a min.'

She was already out of bed and changing into clothes by the time Mr James had told her to hurry and bid his farewells. Quickly shoving her hair into a ponytail, she washed her face and grabbed her makeup bag. Hopefully she would be able to grab a taxi at the hotel entrance and do her makeup on the way. Making sure she had her phone and hotel key, she grabbed bag and rushed down to the hotel reception.

'Good morning.' The receptionist smiled much too merry for Clover's liking. 'How can I help?'

'I need a taxi please. Will there be one outside?'

'There should be. However, if there isn't, just come back in and we'll call on for you.'

'Great. Thanks.' Clover replied quickly before turning to rush off.

'Oh. Excuse me.' The receptionist called her back. 'I almost forgot. You were left this last night.'

Clover headed back to the receptionist, where she was handed an envelope with her name on. Shoving it into her already full bag, she rushed out into the street, where luck would have it a taxi was waiting.

'The courthouse please.' Clover puffed, as she climbed into the back.

Rushing into the waiting room, Clover found Mr James impatiently pacing the room looking at his watch.

'Sorry, sorry.' Clover said without any hesitation. She'd made it with five minutes to spare. Considering she had only been up not even twenty minutes, she thought she'd done quite well. However, it's not something she wanted to admit to Mr James.

'I got you a coffee.' He eyed her suspiciously as he placed the white paper cup with a red lid in front of her, before grabbing a brown-wrapped cereal bar and pushing it across the table.

Clover smiled up at him, thanking him softly and breaking the tension in the room.

'Are you ready? We don't have long.' He looked at his watch again, tapping it several times with his index finger.

She nodded, 'Ready as I ever will be. Do you really think the decision will be today?'

He let out a deep sigh, 'I really don't see why not. I don't think there's much more to go over."'

Before either of them could say anything else, they both heard multiple knocks on the door and watched as it slowly opened, revealing the assistant who gestured them to follow him into the courtroom.

'Welcome everyone.' The judge greeted the room once everyone was silent. 'Over the last two days we have seen two sides of a story. We have seen evidence to support those sides and have also had witnesses in to give their own accounts. The panel have decided that we have seen enough, but before we begin, I need to ask; Does any party have any new evidence to bring to court?'

Mr James answered with a no straight away, but hushed whispers caught everyone's attention from Robs team. It looked like he was in a predicament with his solicitor, but she couldn't quite hear what was being said.

'A decision please.' The judge announced, making them both look up.

'No further evidence.' Robs solicitor announced, causing Rob to cast a disapproving look.

'Very well. I will now address the Jury.'

Clover sat while the judge went over all the finer details of the last two days. She detailed everything that Mr James had pleaded and equally everything which had come from Robs side. She reminded them of evidence which had been given and witnesses which had been questioned. Clover watched as the jury scribbled and made notes in front of them. Trying to read their reactions but failing.

'And with that.' Concluded the judge. 'It is now time for the jury to leave the room. The court will be adjourned until the Jury have made their decision. The time is now 10.45am, so I say we will reconvene at 1pm. Will that be, ok?'

The jury all nodded before gathering up their belongings and exiting the room.

More hushed whisperings came from Robs side, and the judge had to interrupt them with her gavel, as she ended the court.

'What do we do now?' Clover whispered as she followed Mr James out of the room.

'We wait.'

'No, I mean, what do we do now. As in precisely this moment. Do we need to wait here?'

'No. I don't see why not.' He sat down at a table and opened one his files. 'As long as you're back for 1pm, it should be fine to leave.'

'What are you going to do?' Clover eyed the papers he was shuffling through. 'You don't need to go over them surely?'

'I'll just stay here; Harper sent me some files he wanted me to look over for another case.'

'Right.' Clover replied, wondering if he ever stopped working. 'Well, I think I might just head back to the hotel and pack my things. I'll get my car ready, so I can leave as soon as it done.'

'Very well.' Mr James replied, head still focused on the papers in front of him. 'Just be back in time.'

※※※※※

Clover returned in plenty of time, she even had enough time to pop to the local bakers and grab some pastries for her and Mr James.

He smiled as she walked into the room, his cheese sandwich unwrapped next to him.

'You're back.' He announced, as if he wasn't expecting her.

'Of course.' She smiled back at him. 'I've brought you something too, for after you've had your dinner.'

She placed the pastries on the table, next to where he was working. Quickly glancing at the papers, he was working on, she noticed Hope Cottage as the address details. Mr James was too quick and hastily gathered up the papers and placed them back into the folder.

'I wonder what's happening with the jury.' Clover casually changed the subject, acting that she wasn't curious at all what the new owners of Hope Cottage were up to. She doubted very much she would return.

'I think they'll find it very straight forward. Hearing the judge this morning detailing everything, I don't see how they could find it difficult.'

'Hopefully.'

Clover didn't want to get her hopes up too much. But Robs side hadn't been as strong as theirs seemed to be.

'What are your plans after this?'

'Well, if I win, then I have an air B 'n' B booked, down in Cornwall. I'll stay for a couple of weeks and figure out what to do next.' Clover explained. 'If I don't win, then I'll no other option than to move back in with my mum in Glen Peaks.'

Mr James nodded, then glanced at his watch.

'Suppose we better get ready to go and see what happens then.'

They both gathered up their belongings and made their way into the court room. Clover glanced over at Rob's side and noticed everyone's face were a mix of anger and nerves. She also turned around, for the first time to see the rest of the public sitting behind her. Taking in their faces, she spotted Rachel who cast her an awful glare, before turning away. Quiet hushes echoed across the room as the Judge made her way into the room.

'All stand please.' An announcement was made, and everyone stood until being told otherwise.

'Good afternoon, everyone.' The judge greeted the room. 'Before we sit, I'd like to invite the jury back into the room.'

Clover watched as the door was opened and the jury took their places in the jury panel at the side.

'All seat please.'

The rustling of everyone sitting back down echoed across the room and the judge waited for complete silence before addressing the jury.

'Jury, have you reached a decision?'

'We have.' The foreperson for the jury announced aloud to the room.

'Very well. You have been brought here today to reveal your conclusion on this case. This case where Mrs Taylor is suing her husband Mr Taylor on accountants of slander. You have heard Mr Taylor give accounts with witnesses where he was abused both emotionally and verbally by Mrs Taylor. You have heard how he had no other choice but to give his side of the story to the public press. This has not only ruined Mrs Taylors reputation, but it has also stopped her from working.

On the other hand, you have heard accountants from Mrs Taylor defending herself on the statements Mr Taylor has issued. You have seen evidence of Mr Taylor spreading malicious lies to ruin her career. Today we must conclude. Jury, please come forward and announce to the court – How do you find Mrs Taylor?'

Clover stomach whirled with nerves and her palms were sweaty. These people who didn't know her, were about to say one word that could change her life either way.

'Innocent.' The foreperson spoke aloud.

Mr James grinned but kept his calm.

'Now, can you tell me how you find Mr Taylor.'

'Guilty.' The foreperson spoke.

Clover heard gasps from the crowd behind her, quickly followed by a rustling, footsteps, and the door closing. Looking behind her, she noticed Rachel had quickly left the room.

'And that is the closing of the case. I hereby conclude that Mrs Taylor has won this case. Therefore, as agreed prior to this court case. A sum of 1.3 million pound will be awarded to Mrs Taylor, from Mr Taylor in payment of damages. The court can now be dismissed.'

Clover didn't even look over to Rob. She really hoped that this would be the last she would see of him. Following Mr James out of the room, she couldn't wait to get out of there completely.

'Thank you so so much.' Her screech of joy echoed off the walls and filled the room. Mr James smiled, blue eyes twinkling, as if he wanted nothing more than for her to be cheerful in that moment. She felt like she could barely contain her excitement and kept having to resist the urge to leap into the air and shout from the rooftops.

'It's my pleasure.' He replied, smiling at her. 'And if there's anything you need in the future, you know where I am.'

'Absolutely.'

They walked side by side, and as they opened the doors to exit the building, the press were already waiting. Calling her name, finally deciding that they now want to tell her story.

Clover ignored them as she pushed her way through. 'I'll be seeing you then. And really thank you again.'

'It's really no problem at all.'

Mr James waved her off, as she climbed into her car. Her favourite songs on high, she drove into the sunset not knowing what was to come next.

Forty-Eight

Standing alone on the cliffs of Cornwall, Clover closed her eyes and spread her arms wide. The wind off the sea pushed against her skin. She drew a lungful of salty air deep into her lungs then exhaled, letting all thought fall from her mind. Clover felt a wave of relief wash over her as she took the deep breath. She had left the courthouse with only a small bag of belongings that morning and called her mother straight away to explain everything.

'I'm so pleased for you, I really am.' Her mothers voice brought tears to her eyes. 'Hopefully you'll come back and visit soon?'

'One day mum, one day.' Clover replied. 'I think I'll do some travelling first.'

Feeling the warmth of the sun on her face, she looked up from her toes to the horizon, then turned and made her way up the beach. Her eyes lit up when they fell on a small blue van with "Pizza Takeout" written in bold white letters. For once, she felt comfortable in her own skin and wasn't afraid to be around people. She stepped closer and smiled at the teenage boy behind the counter.

'Just the pizza special.' She asked.

'£12.99 please.'

She rooted around in her bag, pushing aside the lipstick and phone until at last, she found her purse. As she pulled it out, an envelope slid from beneath it and landed near her feet. She recognized it immediately—it was the one the hotel receptionist had given to her earlier that morning. She stuffed it back into the bag before taking out her credit card to pay for dinner.   'Take a seat and someone will bring it over to you.'

Clover spotted an empty picnic bench tucked away between two mounds of sand dunes, with a stunning view looking out to the horizon. Taking a seat, she ran her fingers along the envelope in her hands. With trembling fingers, she quickly ripped it open and unfolded the piece of paper inside.

Clover,
I know you didn't want to hear it, but I need to say it. I'm sorry. I'm sorry for hurting you, for judging you when I of all people should have known better. I'm sorry I made you feel like the one person you thought you could trust had let you down. I've been there, I've been that person and I know how it feels. For me to know that I made someone else feel like that is awful and to know it was you who I made feel like that is even worse. I came to find you because I miss you. I miss the way you make me feel, the way you make me laugh, the way you make me feel like anything is possible. There's so much I want to do in life, and I only want to do them things with you. I know you say we've moved on; I know you don't want to talk about what happened or hear my apology. But if I don't do this, then I'll never be able to forgive myself.
Whatever the outcome of the case, just know that I am always here for you, whether its tomorrow or in 10 years' time. I am and always will be yours.
Ed xxx

Clover's gaze was fixated on the letter as she folded it up, her heart breaking into a million pieces. Tears welled up in her eyes and blurred her vision, but she blinked them away quickly before tucking the note into her pocket. She stood up slowly to collect the pizza she had ordered, the heat radiating from the takeout boxes warm against her hands. Taking one last breath, she made her way back to the car park and opened the driver's door to her car. As she pulled out of the car park and onto the open road, Clover followed her heart and drove towards Glen peaks.

Forty-Nine

Clover felt the rumble of the road through her chest as she drove to Glen Peaks. With a quick glance in the rear-view mirror, she saw bags under her eyes – evidence of her ten hours on the road. She knew every corner of this town like the back of her hand and was relieved when at last she spotted the wooden sign that read 'Welcome to Glen Peaks'. The night sky hummed with crickets and locusts, broken only by an occasional mew from a stray cat out scavenging for food. All the lights were off, leaving even the most bustling streets deserted – yet it still felt like home. Pulling over into a side road, she turned off her engine. Taking a deep breath, Clover reclined her seat slightly, closed her eyes, and began to think about what she should do next.

The tapping on her car window jolted her awake. As she squinted against the morning sunlight to make out its source, she realized it was Jack from Glen Peaks. His face was pressed up against the glass with a broad smile. Her heart raced as she fumbled for the keys to start her car and wind down the window.   'Say, what you doing sleeping out here? You got no bed or somethin'?'

Clover smiled at him, trying to suppress a small laugh. She'd never felt so pleased to see the regulars.

'Didn't want to wake anyone. I got in late.' Clover replied.

'Well, he's open now.'

'Who?'

'Ed.' Jack announced louder. 'I said he's open now.'

Clover watched through the window as the old man slowly shuffled down the street. She reached over to the passenger seat and grabbed a bottle of water, twisting off the cap and taking a long sip.

Her mouth felt dry, and she leaned forward on the steering wheel, letting out a deep sigh as her mind raced with thoughts of what was to come. Taking a few moments to gather her courage, Clover opened the car door and stepped onto the sidewalk. As she rounded the corner, she could see one of the locals exiting the shop. The woman noticed Clover and gave a friendly hello. 'Morning lovely,' she said before continuing.   Clover stood outside the shop front, peering through its large picture windows. The shop was empty; Ed wasn't there. Nerves twisted in her stomach as she pushed open the door. The familiar tinkling of the bell above the door alerting that it had been opened sounded. She heard him before she saw him – his voice boomed from the back room, echoing off the tiled walls of the kitchen.

'I'll be out in a minute.'
Clover took a few tentative steps inside as he appeared from behind a doorway, still wiping his hands on an old cloth. He pulled up short when he saw Clover and dropped the towel quickly on the countertop, surprise flickering across his features.
Clover couldn't find any words but that didn't matter -before she knew it her feet had propelled her forward, into his arms. Their kiss was unlike anything they'd ever shared before - full of emotion and longing - and when they finally parted, Ed's beaming smile let Clover know that everything was going to be alright.   'Hi.' She said when they finally pulled apart, a smile plastered across Ed's face made her know that everything was going to be all right.

'Hi.' He replied again. 'What are you doing here?'

'I wanted to come home.' Clover replied honestly, giggling at the outcome she never expected.

'Well, Welcome home.' Ed grinned back, before leaning over and kissing her again.

The shop door opening broke them apart, and Clover busied herself while Ed served the customer. Once the customer had left, Ed quickly scribbled a note on a piece of paper and taped it to the door. *'Back soon.'* It read.

'Come on.' He grabbed Clover's hand and pulled her towards the shop door.

'Where are we going?' she quizzed, letting him guide her.

'Now your home, I want to show you something. Have you got your car?'

'Yes, it's round the side.'

'Give me your keys, I'll drive.'

They made their way to Clover's car, where Ed took the keys and climbed into the driver's seat. Clover opened the passenger door and picked up the pizza box that she'd left on the passenger seat.

'What's that?' Ed asked.

'Pizza.' Clover giggled. 'All the way from Cornwall.'

'Now that needs an explanation.' Ed started the car and pulled away, heading down into the main village of Glen Peaks. They passed Clovers mums house, which reminded Clover that she needed to let her mum know she was home. Out of the town, they headed up the hill and Clover saw Hope Cottage standing proudly on the hill. A sadness overcame her, but she knew she would have to overcome it if she was to remain living here.

'Where are we going?' she asked Ed again.

'Nearly there.' Ed replied, and within seconds he was indicating left, pulling into the driveway of Hope Cottage.

'What are we doing?' Clover gasped, worrying that the new owners would come rushing out telling them to get off their land.

'Get out.' Ed smiled, as he turned off the ignition and climbed out of the car himself. He was already opening the garden gate and heading up the garden path before Clover had even unbuckled her belt. As quick as she could, she hurried after him.

By the time she'd caught up with him, he was stood at the door, as if ready to knock and announce that Clover had come home.

'What are you doing?' Clover whispered, so nobody could hear her.

Ed stood opposite her and took both of her hands in his.

'Welcome home.' Ed grinned at her.

'What do you mean?' Clover whispered once more.

'I brought it.' He was like a child on Christmas day revealing a major surprise gift. 'I brought it for us.'

'What do you mean?' Clover asked again, confused by just what was happening.

'Either way, I knew letting go of Hope Cottage was the last thing you wanted. I knew how much it meant to you, so the minute it went up for sale. I brought it. Hoping that one day you'd come home.'

'You're the buyer?' Clover gasped in shock. 'But how?'

'That's for me to worry about.' Ed reassured. 'But come on, I've got so much to show you.'

He handed her the key, where he urged her to open the front door. Inside he had carried on with the full renovations. The hallway had the original flooring restored, with a living room leading off it. A huge log burner took centre stage in the room, surrounding by neutral but tasteful chesterfield sofas. The kitchen and dining room had been knocked through, creating one big living space. Clover could already see herself and Ed cooking their evening meals together here, while sharing a glass of wine. Barn style doors opened into the garden, where Clover took in all the finer details she'd missed just previously as she rushed through the garden. Flower beds were pristine with seasonal flowers blooming in their prime spots.

'There's something else I'd love you to see.' Ed took her hand and rushed her down to the bottom of the garden, where the stream separated the house and the orchard. The orchard she'd once had big dreams for. Over the bridge, a wooden sign engraved with the wording 'Clover Fields' now hung neatly from a branch which hung over the stream.

'Clover Fields?' Clover quizzed.

Ed grinned, as he continued to guide her over the bridge and over the stile.

Clover took one look at the other side and gasped in shock.

'Oh my gosh Ed. This is amazing.'

The scrawny trees that were there when she first found the orchard were now in full bloom. Creating a tunnel which seemed to go on for miles. She followed Ed through them, amazed with how much he had managed to carry out.

'When I brought the house.' Ed finally began to explain. 'Once all the surveys were done and the deeds were transferred, I realised that the land which Hope Cottage owns expands much more than I think you even knew.'

'What do you mean?'

'We're nearly there.' Clover followed him, just as the trees ended, she saw a huge expanse of freshly mowed field.

'All of this.' Ed spread out his arms to explain. 'Also belongs to Hope Cottage. When the house purchase went through, I thought for days upon days what this space could be put to beneficial use for. And that's when I came up with the idea of Clover Fields.'

'Clover Fields?' Clover felt that all she'd done since she'd got here, was repeat everything Ed was saying.

'Clover Fields.' Ed repeated. 'A glamping field. We'll hire out bell tents, safari tents, glamping pots. Whatever we can get, and people can come to Clover Fields for the ultimate glamping experience. We can sell produce from the orchard, maybe get some chickens like you said. An organic camping farm. I've been talking to lots of advisors, and we'd just need to provide a toilet and shower area for them, but other than that we're good to go.'

Clover stood a gasp; Ed had clearly been terribly busy since she'd been away.

'What do you think?' He waited eagerly for her reply, as she stood and looked around. The field certainly had potential and Clover could see Ed's idea forming already.

'I think it sounds perfect.' Clover grinned. 'And once my payment comes through, I can help fund anything you need.'

'Wait what?' Ed gasped, completely forgetting about the court case. 'You won?'

'We won.' Clover shouted, for the first time finally being able to realise the joy that came with it. 'We won!'

Ed picked her up and spun her round, before placing her firmly back on the ground and kissing her.

'I don't want to ruin the moment.' Clover laughed. 'But I could really do with brushing my teeth, and we've got pizza from Cornwall to eat.'

Ed laughed and ran as he chased Clover back to the house. Back to their home. Back to Hope Cottage.

The End

Thank you for taking the time to read Clover. I hope you enjoyed reading the story of Clover as much I did writing it!

Any feedback or reviews would be gratefully received and can be left either on Amazon or find me on goodreads!

Barbra